"Back in town so soon?" Cooper asked.

"I got laid off, so I'm moving back home and taking that job at the high school," Elise replied.

"Sorry to hear that."

"Sorry to hear I got laid off or sorry to hear I'm moving back home?"

"Laid off. It's not easy making a change. Up until a year ago, I worked in Moab, Utah. I was just beginning to make a life for myself."

"You came because your family needed you," Elise pointed out.

"Didn't make it any easier."

"You're right. But there is no other work. I spent the last month checking out the job market."

"So, Apache Creek High School is your only option?"

The wind picked up, blowing her hair across her face. "It's the option I'm accepting." Cooper tried not to let it bother him that Apache Creek was a last resort. The Elise he knew had loved it here. It was wrong that Elise didn't feel excited about moving back home.

Just as much as i
to walk away fro
planned.

Pamela Tracy is a *USA TODAY* bestselling author who lives with her husband (the inspiration for most of her heroes) and son (the interference for most of her writing time). Since 1999, she has published more than twenty-five books and sold more than a million copies. She's a past RITA® Award finalist and past winner of the American Christian Fiction Writers' Book of the Year Award.

Books by Pamela Tracy

Love Inspired

The Rancher's Daughters

Finally a Hero
Second Chance Christmas

Daddy for Keeps
Once Upon a Cowboy
Once Upon a Christmas

Love Inspired Suspense

Pursuit of Justice
The Price of Redemption
Broken Lullaby
Fugitive Family
Clandestine Cover-Up

Second Chance Christmas

Pamela Tracy

Recycling programs
for this product may
not exist in your area.

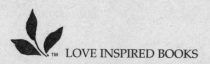 LOVE INSPIRED BOOKS

ISBN-13: 978-0-373-71926-6

Second Chance Christmas

Copyright © 2015 by Pamela Tracy Osback

www.Harlequin.com

Printed in U.S.A.

The heart of man plans his way,
but the Lord establishes his steps.
—*Proverbs* 16:9

To my niece Shannon Leutkenhaus,
a champion team roper, who is living the dream
and has the saddles and buckles to prove it.
Shannon, you rock!

Chapter One

Storm clouds rolled in the Arizona sky, a black-and-gray blanket that sank lower even as Cooper Smith watched. One drop hit his forehead. He whooped, then turned and headed inside his store, AJ's Outfitters. His cell phone was out and in his hand before he made it to the counter. He had five regulars who went gold-panning with him on the Superstition after every rain. Plus, this trip, he had three other numbers to call: tourists who had come into his store to buy expedition gear and had shown an interest in going panning. That meant paying customers.

Something AJ's sorely needed.

He'd gotten hold of all but two when an incoming call interrupted him.

It wasn't someone wanting to go panning tomorrow. Instead a deep voice, one he recognized well, said, "I just saw your brother doing doughnuts in your truck in the parking lot of the Apache Creek fairgrounds."

Cooper closed his eyes. Lately, it was one thing after another with his little brother and each and every incident landed at Cooper's feet. "You sure it was him?"

It was a stupid question, and Cooper didn't even bother to pray that Jacob Hubrecht was wrong. Still, there was nothing quite like having an elder of the church, and your ex-girlfriend's father, phone you right after you switched the Closed sign to Open.

Cooper's little brother, just turned eighteen and ten years younger but an inch taller, was skipping school again. Just six months to go and the kid would graduate. Maybe.

"Nothing wrong with my vision," Jacob answered. "Even in the rain."

There was nothing wrong with Cooper's, either. He opened his eyes and looked around the store. Only three customers, one family really, and only the four-year-old appeared to be the potential sale. He held a fool's gold necklace in hand. Cost: five dollars.

Business was down, and Cooper was still learning how to manage the storekeeping part of his responsibility instead of just the guide part. Going panning tomorrow meant Garrett had to work the store. Cooper would bring in three hundred dollars from the three tourists. That might just double their Saturday total.

Cooper didn't know what more he could do except pray. Lately, he'd not said any prayers for himself until after amen. Sometimes, before falling into an exhausted sleep, he added an addendum, a simple plea: *Help me, God.*

Last time he'd prayed this much was a good ten months ago.

Mitch Smith, his father, had left a big hole to fill when he'd passed away in February, and the hole looked to be getting deeper as the first Christmas without him loomed less than five weeks away.

"I'm sure it was Garrett," Jacob said. "And, it gets worse."

Worse than skipping school and abusing a 1962 classic Ford F-100, four-by-four, V8, four-speed transmission in the rain? Cooper had had a customer offer him five thousand for it two weeks ago, and Cooper had turned him down. They didn't need the money that badly.

Yet.

Cooper didn't want to know how worse his brother was making it. Each passing day just proved to him that he couldn't fill his father's shoes.

Jacob interrupted Cooper's meandering thoughts by sharing, "He had three other teens in the truck with him."

"Great," Cooper muttered. "One is probably David Cagnalia, right?"

"Pretty sure," Jacob agreed. "Plus, two girls I didn't recognize."

Girls? Oh, please no.

"Thanks, Jacob. I appreciate the call. You wouldn't by any chance have some advice on how I should deal with this, would you?"

Jacob Hubrecht had brought up three girls, pretty much on his own, and they'd all turned out perfect. Especially his middle daughter, Elise, who Cooper had been in love with from fourth grade until… Well, Cooper couldn't rightly say that he'd fallen out of love with Elise; it was more as if they'd fallen apart, literally and figuratively.

"Do what you're doing. Keep letting him know you're there. Also, when he decides to talk, listen."

"I've been doing that." Cooper watched his three

customers leave the store without the five-dollar fool's gold necklace. They ran to their car, looking at the sky as if amazed at the Arizona rain. Some storekeeper he was, on the phone the whole time.

"Go fetch Garrett now," Jacob said, grabbing Cooper's attention again. "Get him to school. He'll only be two hours late. Wait to talk to him until tonight when you're not so mad. Better yet, let your mother do the talking."

"I don't know," Cooper said slowly, even as he was thinking how much easier it would be on him if he could let his mother deal with Garrett. "She's not feeling well."

She hadn't felt well since the funeral nine months ago.

"I'll ask Elise if she has any ideas," Jacob said.

Cooper opened his mouth to say "Not necessary", but Jacob wasn't finished. Quickly and proudly, he announced, "She's interviewing today at the high school for some kind of social worker position."

Elise was coming home.

After a decade.

Home.

But not to him.

"No, thanks," Cooper said. "I'll handle it on my own."

Elise Hubrecht had never been a fan of the term *last resort*. Unfortunately, she wasn't a fan of the word *unemployed*, either. Just the thought of it gave her an upset stomach. She had a school loan, more than one credit card and daily bills. If she moved back to Apache Creek, she could live at the ranch for a while, maybe pay off the credit cards and buy a new truck—new to her, anyways. The way things were going, her old truck wouldn't last much longer. It hadn't started this morning, so she was in one of her dad's Lost Dutchman Ranch trucks, which had brought back memories of high school. All her best memories were here, in Apache Creek, Arizona.

And her worst memories, too. Those were why she had left, ten years ago. And why she hadn't planned to return.

Her father, who claimed he didn't have an emotional side, had all but killed the fatted calf when she'd told him she was coming home for a job interview. She had an eleven o'clock appointment with Principal Beecher and a few school board members who made up the hiring committee. Checking her watch, she figured she'd be a good twenty minutes early. For no other reason than curiosity, she turned left when she should have turned right, and headed down the rural road to AJ's Outfitters.

She passed the weathered white brick building with its dark blue roof. Odd, there was a Closed sign on the door. It was a Friday morning, late November. Perfect weather and the busy season for the Arizona outdoorsmen.

None of her business. She pressed on the gas and drove toward the street that eventually lead to the high school. She cracked the window and took a deep breath of the eighty-degree Arizona winter.

Just two blocks from the school, she caught sight of a red truck moving fast off-road, to her left, and bumping crazily on terrain never meant for tires. Then it abruptly turned and traveled down a fairly steep embankment.

Elise blinked. She recognized the vehicle.

The driver didn't even hesitate when he swerved in front of her truck, skidding slightly on the pavement, and finally straightening. Then the driver hit the gas and turned down the road that led right toward her family's ranch.

The Cooper she remembered drove slower than her great-uncle and never broke the law. Couldn't be him. Besides, the momentary glance she'd managed into the front seat of the red truck highlighted what looked like four teenagers, all laughing, maybe screaming, but definitely younger than Cooper and his friends.

More the age of Cooper's much younger brother. She'd seen Garrett briefly at his father's funeral back in February. Elise made a snap decision, turned to follow, all the while knowing she was getting involved and that would only make her even more desirable to the school board that so desperately wanted to hire her.

If only Mike Hamm, her favorite minister and now apparently a member of the school board, hadn't seen her résumé posted on a job-hunting website and called her with an offer. It was the only job available for five hundred miles. She knew this. But coming home felt like such a step back—from everything she'd accomplished in her current home of Two Mules, Arizona, and everything she'd hoped to achieve there in the next few years.

She'd just been starting to make headway with some of the local teens. Her work there was supposed to make up for her failures in the past. She couldn't walk away now. Especially not to come back here—the site of those painful failures.

What she really couldn't seem to do was stop following Cooper's truck even as it veered from one side of the road to the other. It was an accident waiting to happen and she the only witness. Where was everyone?

The truck in front of her turned again, Elise on its tail. She'd be late for her interview, that was for sure, but clearly the teens in front of her needed a reality check.

The truck careened across the dirt road and into the remnants of Karl Wilcox's cotton field. When she was a teen, Mr. Wilcox owned a shotgun, which he filled with buckshot and was quite willing to use on anyone who messed with his land. She doubted that had changed in the years since then.

Elise honked her horn, trying to get the teens to pull over. It took a good five minutes, time Elise spent with her cell phone aimed out the window taking a video. She knew a picture was worth a thousand words, especially when parents wanted denial more than truth. Finally Elise cornered them when a dirt road they'd turned on dead-ended. She stepped out of her vehicle and waited, noting that a rainbow had already formed above the Superstition Mountains that towered over the landscape.

A tall brown-haired boy stepped from the vehicle. Her breath caught. Cooper ten years ago.

"Garrett," she said. "I just took a video of your little adventure with my cell phone."

He blinked as recognition set in. "Does Cooper know you're here?"

"No, but we can talk about that later. I'm on my way to speak with Principal Beecher about a job opening. That makes it very convenient to just follow you four to school. That's where you were heading, right?"

She worded it carefully, hoping they'd realize that a *Yes* answer might mean fewer consequences. From where Elise stood, she could see relief on the girls' faces. The boy standing by the red truck never changed his angry expression. As for Garrett, he merely nodded his head, lips pressed together, and then marched back to his truck.

"Get in," he told his friends. After a deliberate few seconds making a point, they crawled in the front seat.

Later, slightly late and a little damp from the rain, Elise sat at a conference table and studied the three men sitting across from her. The principal of Apache Creek High, David Beecher, still looked annoyed. Not at her, but at the four seniors who'd showed up right behind her late to school and with an escort. They were now with the vice principal.

She hoped that on their own the teens owned up to their responsibility, not just about ditching school but about where they'd been and what they'd done. Wilcox's cotton field was pretty much destroyed.

She hadn't shared with the principal the lack of respect shown by the two boys when she'd mentioned showing her video to their families. Not without knowing more about the situation.

Of the four teens, she only knew the background of one, and she remembered him at age seven or eight, building a tree house in the backyard, a place where he and his friends could play their handheld electronics without being disturbed. He'd had a slight crush on her, and oh how big brother Cooper liked to tease. She wanted to believe that sweet kid was still there inside that surly teen.

"Tell me again what you saw," Mike Hamm asked.

"I recognized the trunk and knew Cooper wasn't driving. It was easy enough to figure out they weren't on their way to school," Elise said. "I followed, managed to get them to pull over, and suggested a tardy would be better than an absence."

"Good thinking. I hope there's someone like you around when my children get to high school." Mike had two children, both under the age of three. He had a while before he needed to worry. She, however, knew what he was doing. He was letting her know how very much she was needed here.

She knew she was right when he leaned forward, hands folded in front of him, a sincere expression on his face. "Situations like these are why we petitioned for funding to hire a guidance counselor."

"We have a school counselor," Beecher said, "but quite honestly, she knows more about getting kids on track for college than on getting them back on track for life."

"Miss Sadie's still here?" Elise asked.

"For three more years." The principal smiled as if he'd heard the threat before. Miss Sadie had been advising students of future opportunities since Elise's mom had been a student.

"Once the funding came through for a school counselor, Mike found your résumé online and we read about what you've been doing up in Two Mules." This came from an imposing man who sat on Mike's left, and the only one Elise didn't know from her years growing up in the area. Mike had introduced him as the new chief of police, Ethan Fisher.

The principal nodded before adding, "Three new teen programs in under a year."

That I'm still developing, she thought but didn't say.

"Your résumé is impressive," Mike said. "But we didn't think we were looking for a social worker. Then we started looking at the successes happening where schools employ one."

"Of course, those schools are a lot bigger and have more tax dollars and such. We would need you to wear a couple of hats," Principal Beecher said. "You'd not only be a social worker dealing with crisis intervention within the school walls but also working outside the school with families and the communities."

In Two Mules she'd had to make time for academic emphasis. Apache Creek was dictating the emphasis. On the table before her was her dream job. But why did it have to happen now, when her work in Two Mules— the work that was supposed to make up for her past— was still unfinished?

Principal Beecher opened a manila folder and withdrew some papers. "We've changed the job description a bit since Mike spoke to you. And we were able to raise the pay so it matches what you make now."

Almost as if they were bidden, her fingers slid across the table and took the papers. She still wanted to say no—but her justifications were melting away. Yes, she'd be two hours away from Two Mules, but she could live at the Lost Dutchman and save on rent. She'd easily be able to afford gas back and forth to visit often. Once a week, she could manage that. She'd find the time. That had been her mantra since Cindy died. To always make time for someone who needed her.

"Jasmine Taylor ran away just over a month ago," Principal Beecher said. "Three months into the school semester. It's all the seniors can talk about. I hear from parents almost daily. They're all worried that their sons and daughters might run away, too."

Elise remembered Jasmine as a seven-year-old

brown-haired girl who hated it when her big sister baby-sat. Elise had been over there a time or two, riding horses in their back field and playing. Jasmine would be sixteen or seventeen now. Close to Garrett's age. She wasn't one of the teens Elise had so diligently mentored in Two Mules...but she was still a girl in trouble. A girl Elise might be able to help. "Any word from her at all?" Elise asked. She tried to settle back in her black, hard plastic chair and looked at the photos and certificates on the wall. A college diploma or two. Photos of winning football teams, debate teams and cheerleaders. She recognized Cooper, bent on one knee, in the front row of the football photo just over the principal's head.

Mike answered, "No, no sightings, no cryptic messages to her parents."

Mike Hamm touched the screen of his iPad. "Also, David Cagnalia shoplifted at a convenience store near the interstate a month ago. They caught him on the outskirts of town."

"Sounds like a call for help." Elise rubbed her temples. She'd been told that David was the other young man in Garrett's truck.

Above the principal's head and slightly to the left was a photo of her and Cooper taken after they'd become the first Apache Creek students to win the Arizona High School Rodeo Team Roping Competition. "You still sending students to the rodeo competition?" Elise asked.

"Not since your little sister graduated and your dad no longer ran the program. There's no one with time and rodeo experience to spearhead an after-school program now."

Elise's father had started the program when Elise's older sister, Eva, was a freshman, hoping to get her involved and overcome her fear of horses. By the time he realized his ploy wasn't going to work, he had twenty students counting on him. When Elise started her freshman year, Apache Creek High School was making a name for itself in the competition arena. When baby sister Emily entered, parents were filling out vouchers and driving their kids fifty miles to attend a school out of district just so they could be under her father's tutelage. The saddle came easy to Emily but it wasn't her calling. Still, she boasted a few buckles herself.

"The last three years the number of incidents involving teenagers in Apache Creek has increased two hundred percent," Ethan Fisher said.

"It's an epidemic, kids running away and skipping school, girls getting pregnant before they graduate, and boys," the principal choked up, "boys making decisions that will go on their record. David is a senior, and he's nineteen."

It was the catch in the principal's voice, the look in the police chief's eyes and Mike Hamm's hands folded in prayer that spurred Elise to say words she couldn't possibly mean.

No way could she return to Apache Creek to live.

No way.

"I'll know by next week if my job in Two Mules has been eliminated. Are you willing to wait that long?"

"That would be fine," Principal Beecher said. "We can get busy with the paperwork." The men talked a bit longer, about pay and hours and benefits.

Elise stared at the photo of her and Cooper on the wall, remembering a past that warred with the present and colored the future.

Chapter Two

After she'd shaken hands with the chief of police and principal for the second time, she followed Mike out the door and into the hallway. It was almost Thanksgiving, but backpacks still looked new, maybe because no one took books home; jeans still looked purposely old, maybe because kids bought them that way; and no one looked exhausted. The hallway pulsed with teenage angst and smelled like a combination cafeteria and gym with a hint of perfume.

"You need to come home." Mike led the way down the stairs to the exit and to the parking lot. Apache Creek High School hadn't changed much since Elise had graduated, except maybe to be a bit smaller.

When they got to her truck, Elise closed her eyes as she leaned against the hood. "Mike, I appreciate you reaching out to me, but—"

"Think of it as a plea for help. You can make a difference, more than anyone I know."

"I don't think I'm strong enough," Elise whispered.

"You're stronger than any girl I know," Mike said. "I know you don't like talking about Cindy, but from the time you two were in kindergarten, you were a person that she always wanted to be with. You made a difference with her, just like you'll do with the kids here at the high school. Believe me, I know how her death hurt you. But you couldn't have prevented it. Don't let it keep you from coming home. Apache Creek needs you."

She'd successfully blocked the request to move back home a hundred times the last ten years. She had great reasons, too. The fact that maybe she could have prevented Cindy's death being the main roadblock. She'd always thought she'd come back *someday*—a far off someday when she wasn't weighed down by guilt; when she'd helped enough teens to feel like she'd made amends for not being there for her friend. That "someday" hadn't come yet.

"In many ways," Mike continued, "you're an answer to our prayers."

She'd had a hard time praying lately, for years really. Early on, right after Cindy's funeral, Elise had prayed for forgiveness. It hadn't, in her opinion, come. Maybe she didn't deserve it.

She hadn't done enough to help Cindy, hadn't reacted fast enough to save her. Now, though, she was saving others. Just last month she'd found a local rancher in Two Mules who was willing to let kids come to his place and take riding lessons. Her goal was to get them into competitions, give them something to aim for. She was going to train them the way her father had trained her. She'd show them one walk, trot, canter at a time that they were important and they could shape their future, by taking charge of it.

When she didn't say anything, he implored, "We sure need some help."

Apache Creek needs you.

"The people of Two Mules need me, too," she mentioned casually.

"I hear," Mike said, "that the natural gas pipeline has been completed. You know what the Bible says, in Proverbs."

Trust Mike to have a scripture.

"The heart of man plans his way, but the Lord establishes his steps."

Elise frowned. How did he do that? Just pull a scripture from memory, one that was impossible to argue with. And it just figured he knew about the change in the economy. Two Mules, when she'd started working there, had enough money and cases to keep three social workers busy. Now that the pipeline workers and their families were moving on, Two Mules's newly decreased budget barely had funds for two social workers although it still had a client list that called for four.

Fewer people did not equate to less need.

But the budget would win.

If Elise were let go, her coworkers could keep their jobs. Both were natives of Two Mules. Both had families: kids in school and grandparents to care for. Both were good at their jobs, dedicated, but neither focused on the needs of teens. They were mostly dealing with parolees, destitute families, and self-help programs.

Everything she'd worked for, finally coming to fruition this last year, could fade to nothingness. Even if she went back weekly to visit, would it be enough?

"Sometimes," Mike said gently, "you're most needed in the place that defined you."

He, she knew, felt that way. Ten years ago, he'd been finishing med school. The only one from his family of ten kids to go to college. She'd been a high school senior talking to colleges about a rodeo scholarship. Cooper was doing the exact same thing.

Then Cindy, Mike's little sister and Elise's best friend, died in a car crash caused by Cindy's drunken boyfriend.

Mike had transferred to a Bible college.

Elise had changed her dreams.

A royal blue truck with the Lost Dutchman Ranch logo drove by AJ's Outfitters, slowed down, and then sped up. Cooper Smith stopped listening to the sales pitch coming from his cell phone and watched the truck. He wondered if it were Jacob Hubrecht wanting to stop by and see how Garrett was getting along, if this were a good time.

There was no such thing as a good time anymore. His mother had had a hard time rousing herself from bed to come in this morning to watch the store while Cooper was out looking for his brother.

Luckily, just an hour into the search, the school had called. They were handling it. Garrett wasn't getting suspended. The vice-principal used words like *intervention* and *group meetings* during the phone call, but he hadn't been willing to share anything concrete about the school's disciplinary plans. Cooper wasn't the parent and privacy laws were more stringent than during Cooper's tenure at Apache Creek High School.

There'd be a parent meeting next week. His mom needed to call the man back. He hoped she'd feel up to it.

He turned his attention back to the phone. "Really?" Cooper said. "You do realize that I'm located in Apache

Creek, Arizona. We do have tourists, but honestly we cater to a more serious crowd."

He truly questioned the knowledge of this particular supplier who had called with an offer.

A lame offer.

"Keep in mind," the supplier said, "tourists like to take souvenirs back, and they want something affordable and easy to transport."

"I just don't think practice panning gravel is something that will go over well with my clients." Cooper's biggest complaint about being a storekeeper, aside from it taking time away from his being a guide, was dealing with frivolous details. "No, thanks."

Before the man could continue, Cooper ended the call. Outdoors he could see the shrubs, cacti and an occasional Joshua tree or two that peppered the landscape. In the distance were the Superstition Mountains, looking regal and daring and glistening from the rain.

It seldom rained in November. But this was proving to be the wettest that Cooper could remember. The newspaper claimed Apache Creek was going through a ten-year cycle.

Cooper wanted to be outdoors!

His mother came from the back, slowly opening and closing the fingers of her right hand. "Who was that on the phone?"

He hadn't told her about the call from school. He knew he'd have to eventually—she still needed to set up that parent meeting. But something about the pinched look on her face made him want to protect her for a little while longer. "Just a salesman trying to convince me we needed something we didn't need. Did you hurt your hand?"

"Just some pain in the joints. I dropped a box I was trying to put away."

His mother's hands did look a little swollen and red. She'd been complaining that they felt stiff.

"You need to go to the doctor, Mom. Figure out what's going on."

"It's just age. Speaking of which, I think I'll go home and lie down for a while. We're not busy."

He watched as she headed out of the store and got in her car. She'd come in thirty minutes after he'd re-opened the store.

"Excuse me, do you have a book that's like a biography of someone who spent time mining in the Superstition Mountains?" It wasn't the first time Cooper had heard this request. The man wanted to read about Jacob Waltz, the Lost Dutchman, who'd started the whole "There's a treasure in them hills" mentality.

"Not really."

The customer's face fell. He spent a few minutes going through the books Cooper did have on display and then left, but not before saying, "You need to put out some Christmas decorations or something."

Christmas?

Every time the holiday knocked on Cooper's mind, he refused to open the door. Too busy.

Looking around the shop, he realized the customer was right. Cooper needed to start putting out his yuletide decorations. Dad had always claimed that Santa was a gold panner. He'd needed money to fund his shop and pay the elves, right? And, the North Pole had to have gold. It was in Alaska! Now that would be a reality show. Santa and his elves maneuvering an excavator and suffering make-or-break decisions.

Yes, Thanksgiving might be next week, but turkeys didn't help sales much. But he knew that Christmas trumped every holiday, and the store needed to increase sales so that Cooper's first year as co-owner wasn't his last.

Somehow, he also needed to get Garrett through high school and into college. And then when he'd done all that, maybe he'd cure cancer or institute world peace. Those tasks couldn't seem any more difficult than the ones ahead of him now.

Putting his phone in his shirt pocket, Cooper went back to work. He'd had goals for today before Garrett interrupted them. He started counting his supply of metal detectors. His most expensive kit was over two thousand; his cheapest came in at two hundred. That was on sale.

He hadn't sold one in over two weeks. How many customers had he missed while out looking for Garrett?

He checked his list for tomorrow's outing. He had eight; he needed ten; he could handle fifteen. Five of the people signed up were teenagers from his church. He didn't charge them. The three tourists would be a boost, but he wished there were more of them.

Outside, gravel crunched as another customer pulled into the parking lot. Cooper paused, metal detector in hand, almost like a weapon. It was back, the Lost Dutchman's royal blue Ford truck.

The sight of one—and old Jacob Hubrecht probably owned four—always made Cooper Smith want to run out the front door and shout, "Wait for me!" Ten years ago, he hadn't run fast enough, shouted loud enough, and Elise Hubrecht had driven away without a backward glance or goodbye, taking his heart with her.

Since that day, the sight of a blue Lost Dutchman truck in his parking lot meant one of Elise's sisters or her dad. Today, judging by the brown-haired boy scrambling out of the passenger-side door, he'd be dealing with Eva, Elise's big sister, and Eva's stepson, Timmy.

"Hey, Cooper." Timmy smiled as he set off the large brass bell that announced customers entering AJ's Outfitters. The bell was old and annoying, but his father had installed it and Cooper didn't have the heart to replace it.

"What are you doing out and about on a school day?" Cooper asked.

"I had to go to the dentist, and I was so good that Eva said I could sign up for one of your tours up the mountain. I've been askin' and askin' and it's raining so the perfect time. That's what Grandpa said. Did you know that? He says I ride better than most grown-ups and that you'd help me find gold. Can I go tomorrow? Please."

Cooper stared around Timmy, waiting for Eva to finally exit the truck. She'd always been the most organized of the Hubrecht sisters, the thinker and nurturer of the set. She'd been the one who made sure all supplies were packed, who made reminder calls, and who checked the final scoring numbers.

The baby of the family, Emily, didn't care. She knew her big sisters would take care of her. She merely kept track of what was going on, often filming it to post online, and writing about it on some blog or Facebook page she'd started.

Cooper's ex-girlfriend, middle daughter Elise, had been the risk-taker of the sisters. She did the numbers in her head and always knew her rank and position. She thought the fewer supplies the better, and if they happened to forget something, then obviously they'd not needed it. Back then, at least when it counted, he'd been the only thing she needed.

In the end, he'd not been enough.

"Is Eva going to enroll with you or will it be your dad?" Cooper grinned. Eva, everyone knew, was afraid of horses. He'd heard she was doing better, but he doubted she'd be willing to do the ups and downs of the Superstition Mountains. He emphasized *Only Experienced, Confident Riders* for tomorrow's tour. He'd still get a few tenderfoots. Now Timmy's dad, Jesse, was such a good rider that he could probably lead the tour. But Jesse wouldn't know how to talk gold panning.

Eva came through the door, letting a slight breeze in with her. "Jesse says he'll go along. He'll stay once he delivers the horses."

Cooper's family owned five horses and two mules. After his dad died, he'd started boarding all but his quarter horse Percy Jackson at the Lost Dutchman. It was for the best. His mom hadn't ridden in years and Cooper could never convince Garrett to go for a ride anymore. On the other hand, Cooper managed to get at least an hour a day—make that evening—in on PJ. Sometimes he thought the time spent on the back of his horse was all that kept him sane.

That and prayers.

"When are you going to try, Eva?" he queried. "Jesse says you go for a ride with him at least once a week."

"At the rate I'm improving, I'll be ready to ride the mountain when I turn eighty-six."

He'd been about to mention that Elise had done the mountain when she was six. But then the bell rang as the front door opened and Elise stood there.

A small smile curved the lips he'd once called his own. Her hair was longer, caught in a braid. She'd always gone for vibrant colors, but today wore a royal blue two-piece suit and sensible shoes. He preferred her in button-down shirts that tucked into jeans hugging the legs that had chased him across the football field and tackled him.

It was her eyes that made him step back, bump into the shelf holding bucket survival kits. When they looked into his, they didn't light up.

After all these years, why did he still expect it?

"Hey," he said, keeping his tone even. Instinctively, he knew not to head toward her and try to give her the type of hug old friends exchange. It hadn't been a good breakup.

"Hi, Cooper," Elise said.

As if they were merely acquaintances meeting again after a long time.

"Don't tell me," Eva exclaimed, hurrying across the store and giving her a hug. "You took the job!"

"I…" Elise apparently didn't have an answer. Funny, she'd always been as quick-tongued as she was sure-footed. Cooper watched as the two sisters squared off, suddenly certain that life was about to get a whole lot more interesting.

Eva stepped out of the hug, crossed her arms, and encouraged, "You know you're perfect for it."

"That doesn't mean it's perfect for me," Elise finally managed.

Silence, reminding him much of the silence between him and his brother, reigned.

"Hi, Aunt Elise," Timmy jumped in, rescuing them from an awkward moment. "It's raining, so I'm signing up for tomorrow's horseback ride. I'm going to find gold. You should come with us. Eva says you're the best rider in the world."

"The world's a pretty big place." Elise walked the rest of the way into the store and bent down so she was eye level with the boy. "I'm sure there are a few better riders. Cooper here is pretty good, or so I'm told."

Eva laughed. "That's putting it mildly. So, really how did the interview go?"

"I…"

There she went again with the "I…" instead of just spitting out whatever it was.

"What brings you to AJ's Outfitters?" Cooper asked, as if she hadn't been in the store a million times. "You need some mining gear? Must need something special to drive in all the way from Two Mules."

"I'm here for a job interview. I was just at the high school," Elise admitted. "They're thinking about hiring a social worker, and—"

"—you took the job?" Eva was nothing if not persistent.

Elise shot Eva a dirty look. "No, I told them I'd think about it." To Cooper, she said, "It's just that Two Mules will be laying off one of us, and—"

"If you take the job—" Eva got excited all over again "—we'll get to see you more than a few times a year?"

Elise had been in his store over two minutes and not once had acted like he was anything but a storekeeper.

"If you came home, you might have to get close to people again," he commented, working hard to keep his tone casual.

"I'm close to people." She didn't exactly snap at him, but her words had bite. "I'm just committed elsewhere."

Cooper didn't bother to tell her what he thought about her using the word *committed*. At one time, she'd known the meaning of the word. If she'd stayed true to it, they'd have been married four or five years, maybe have a kid or two. Come to think of it. *Committed* had two meanings. Cooper needed to be committed for still harboring feelings for her.

"It would be awesome if you came back home," Eva gushed. "The ranch could use the help. We're busier than ever. And, if you worked at the high school just think of all the good you could do for those kids."

Wisely, Cooper didn't contribute to this train of thought. Maybe Eva was right. He sure knew those kids at the high school needed all the help they could get. But he really wished some other knight—knightess?—in shining armor was showing up. Elise had not been there when Cooper needed her most. He couldn't trust her to be there for Garrett.

Maybe he should look into getting counseling for Garrett. Cooper couldn't imagine going through the trials of being a high school student without his dad being there.

Mitch Smith had been his anchor after Elise left. He'd dogged Cooper, getting him to work more, attend church functions even without Elise on his arm, and finally talked Cooper into putting away the engagement ring and going to college on the rodeo scholarship, only as a solo instead of a pair.

"Best thing you can do," Mitch had advised all those years ago, "is remain a ship in the ocean she'll return to."

His dad had sayings for every occasion.

Cooper's ship had sunk, risen, been attacked a few

times, and now sported a couple of holes. But he was still sailing. Unfortunately, he was now so used to being solo he wasn't sure he wanted the condition to change.

One thing for sure, he couldn't accept Elise as anything but a deserter.

"Hmph." Clearly, Eva wasn't impressed with her sister's evasive responses. "We can talk more tonight."

"I might head back to Two Mules tonight. I've got the dogs to think of, plus I really need—"

"Your next-door neighbors love your dogs. You know they'll take care of them."

Eva turned to Cooper. "If you'll just let me sign Timmy and Jesse up for tomorrow's ride, we'll get going." Turning to Elise, she said, "I'm thinking there's a reason why you're here to see Cooper."

To Cooper's surprise, Elise didn't protest.

"We're having fried chicken," Timmy said. "You'll like it, especially if you use ketchup."

Cooper winked at Timmy and took care of their registration. A moment later, the pair left and he faced Elise alone. If anything, she'd improved with age, more beautiful now than she'd been at sixteen when he'd gotten the courage to ask her out for a real date. Then, he'd had to bolster up the courage to ask her father's permission.

"What can I do for you?" His words broke the silence, and he sounded very much older, detached, businesslike. Good. That's the way he needed to keep it. She clearly didn't want to stay in Apache Creek, which meant she didn't miss the town or him.

"I'm sorry about your dad."

He blinked. Not what he was expecting. She'd come to the funeral, sat in the back, shook his hand and gave him a hug that cold February day. He'd been so numb that he'd let her pretend to be just a distant friend of the family paying tribute.

There was nothing "just" about Elise Hubrecht when it came to Cooper Smith's feelings.

"Thank you, we miss him, but we're doing fine."

He'd always been able to read her—and right now, he could see her skepticism. She didn't exactly raise an eyebrow, but he could tell she wanted to. He kept waiting for her to move. She kept those glittering black eyes that missed nothing fixed on him and asked, "Garrett doing fine?"

"He's having a bit of a hard time," Cooper admitted, "but he's in high school. Not a good time to lose your dad."

He expected her to say there's never a good time. She'd lost her mother when she was in elementary school. Her father found himself raising three girls alone. Many a night Cooper had heard his parents talking about how hard it must be for a man who was used to roping horses to switch to corralling daughters.

Cooper hadn't understood. Now he did, as he watched his brother Garrett turn from a mostly easygoing teen with a typical know-it-all attitude to a teen with a chip on his shoulder and something to prove.

Just what, Cooper hadn't a clue.

"I don't think my news is going to make you happy, but you need to see this, all the same." She came to the counter and set her purse down before digging into its depths. Soon, an iPhone appeared in her hand. It took her only a second to find what she wanted, a video, and then she handed him her phone. He tapped the start arrow and watched as his truck came zooming down a fairly steep incline—where no road existed—and then sped crazily across terrain never meant for tires.

Cooper didn't realize he'd been holding his breath until he watched the footage of his truck destroying a portion of Karl Wilcox's cotton crop. Dimly, Cooper remembered Jacob on the phone saying, "It gets worse." Karl was a legend in the area for not practicing the Love Thy Neighbor mantra. He didn't forgive or forget, at least not during Cooper's lifetime.

"I was on my way to the school for the interview when I came across your brother and his friends."

"And you chased them down and filmed them?"

"I did, and I convinced them to go to school."

"I'm surprised the vice-principal didn't mention that Garrett engaged in a little destruction of property when he was supposed to be in school."

"I didn't share this with any of the school officials." Elise fingered a club advertisement on the counter.

"Why not?"

"I recognized Garrett. I figured maybe you could talk to parents of the other teens in the truck and then visit Mr. Wilcox on your own. I didn't know at the time that David Cagnalia had already been in trouble."

Cooper very much wanted to ban his brother from the likes of David Cagnalia, but one thing held him back. He wasn't sure who the bad influence was: David or Garrett? When David misbehaved, he always got caught. Garrett, however, knew how to be sly. At least with David, Garrett would always get busted.

"What would you recommend I do to Garrett, if, say, you were the school social worker?"

She hesitated. Her eyes sought out his, focusing in, and pulling him in the way she had all those years ago.

He could still see the old Elise, buried under a sadness he didn't know how to penetrate.

"First, he needs to work in Wilcox's field, putting it back to rights along with the others. Then get him involved in group activities. What's happening at the church?"

"No youth minister now. Parents are taking turns organizing events, but everyone's busy. I don't think we've done anything except a game night and that was on the fly. Garrett didn't want to go. I made him."

"School? Does he play football, ride, anything like that?"

"Coach Nelson retired two years ago and Garrett used that as an excuse to drop out of football. He went to one or two basketball practices but then stopped. We've not had a rodeo team since Emily graduated and your dad stepped down. I wish more than anything that Garrett had something like we had."

She didn't even blink.

Maybe she no longer remembered. Maybe she didn't care. But Cooper did. He wished Garrett had a girlfriend who liked to chase him through the fields, only to crash down beside him on the soft grass. Someone to show him that love came in a compact package with long black hair, glittering eyes and a soft touch.

But then again, maybe that wasn't what Garrett needed after all. His brother had already been in a world of hurt for the past year. If he found love, there was a chance it could turn sour on him. And the last thing Garrett needed on top of everything else was a broken heart like Cooper's.

Chapter Three

Breakfast at the Lost Dutchman was huge, designed for the many guests staying at the dude ranch, as was supper. Lunch, however, was on your own or a pre-packaged sandwich-chips-apple combination. It was well past lunchtime, but Fridays usually meant guests arriving after the noon hour, so Cook always had boxed lunches available for sale: her father's idea.

He sat across from her, talking on his cell phone, not so much barking orders as giving advice. He was good at both. Elise listened as her dad advised someone who obviously knew little about ranching to not spend all their money on upgrades.

Her dad did have a certain "either do it yourself or pay it all off before the next venture" kind of attitude.

Her senior year, they'd planned out her college career. If she'd followed his advice, she'd be nearly debt-free by now. But that plan had gone out the window when she'd given up her rodeo scholarship and set out in a whole new direction with her life.

Finally, Dad ended the call and handed her the boxed

lunch he'd brought in. "If you want something else, Cook will make it. He's always had a soft spot for you."

She'd already stopped in the kitchen and gotten her hug.

She pushed the box back toward him. "I'm not really hungry."

As if to prove her wrong, Cook hurried from the kitchen. Slightly stooped, more than chubby, with dark tufts of hair on either side of his head and then a swatch of baldness across the top, he looked exactly the way she remembered him. Cook's real name was David Cook. Thus, he liked being called Cook. He was a great buddy of her father's and traveled the rodeo circuit with him. Back then his nickname had been Tumble.

"I remembered your favorite," he bragged. He plopped the plate in front of her. Two peanut butter, honey and raisin sandwiches, no crust. A few chips spilled from the sides. The only thing missing from her childhood was—

"Would you like a glass of milk?"

"I'd like that very much, Cook."

He nodded, and hurried off.

Her father cleared his throat. "We're always glad when you stop by to visit."

He was trying. She knew that. A man accustomed to being in charge, he hadn't taken it well when she'd broken away from his plans for her. When she'd first moved away, he'd ordered her back. When that didn't work, he'd threatened. And, when that didn't work, he'd cajoled. By that time she was enrolled in school and doing well. He'd admitted defeat, but not gracefully.

"How did the job interview go today?" He leaned

back, a toothpick in his mouth and an attitude of good-ole-boy that worked with everyone but her.

"It went well. If I want the job, it's mine. They gave me a week to decide."

"Any chance Two Mules won't lay you off?"

"No, it's a small office. I figure it's a matter of days, minutes even."

"Will it really be so bad, coming back here to work?"

She thought about it, swallowed and slowly shook her head. How many times had she told a client that the best way to battle the past was to face it? She'd always felt guilty that she was giving advice she didn't follow.

"It's just that I was finally getting more activities for the teenagers. I had the local library doing tutoring and study groups. And—" she looked up at her dad, smiling "—I had a rancher willing to help kids get ready for rodeo competitions." Her dad already knew this. She'd called him a dozen times asking for advice. She continued, "I just know that if the teens had something productive and active to do with their time, they'd not get in so much trouble."

Her dad nodded. "No reason you can't do the same here." Elise didn't answer. Instead, she took a big bite of her sandwich and tried to tame the turmoil in her heart.

"What if I get it started and before fruition, I'm let go? Apache Creek isn't that big. Budget cuts could happen here, too."

"That's not what's keeping you from taking the job." Her father knew her too well. Sitting across from him now, she thought about the years he'd guided her, always giving her a safe place to land. Too many of her kids, her clients, didn't have such a place, let alone a father.

Jacob Hubrecht still had a full head of hair, light

brown and brushed to the side. His eyebrows were bushy, his mouth wide. Age had given him wrinkles, very defined. Age had also, finally, given him patience. He'd always been the bomb going off in a room, setting people scrambling to please him. Now he knew to hold the match, hold off on lighting the fuse, see what might happen.

Elise finished one sandwich and moved on to the next. Across from her, her father was already finished. Some days, he'd finish a box lunch and ask for a second or third. Other times, he grazed all day. She was the same way. It drove Eva nuts. Her big sister, the one who managed the guest services at the Lost Dutchman, was all about rules and schedules: breakfast at eight, lunch available eleven to one, dinner at six. Snacks could be bananas or crackers or something.

"It's part of it," Elise said. "Did you know so many kids are getting in trouble here in Apache Creek? Did you tell them to call me?"

She should have suspected his part before now. He and Mike Hamm were tight.

Dad, however, shook his head. "They called me to see if I thought you'd be willing to move back. I said they should talk to you. Even if you weren't interested in the job, I said they should see exactly what you're doing to find out if we could try it here. I know they've tossed around ideas, everything from hiring a security guard to walk the halls all the way up to instigating some sort of Scared Straight program. Every idea gets shot down."

"Why?"

"At first, it was a money issue. Now, though, I think everyone's willing to find money in the budget. But what's the solution? No one's sure. I don't remember it being this bad when you kids were in school."

"How bad is it?

"Jasmine Taylor ran away. She's only seventeen. Her parents are worried sick, and no one seems to know where she is or why she ran."

Elise said the first thing that came to mind. "Maybe she got pregnant and is afraid to tell her parents."

"She didn't have a boyfriend that they can figure out. She's as shy as a mouse. Her parents say she spent more time on her horse than she did with friends. The police took the family computer and figured out that she did an internet search on running away. Her parents think she both saved and stole about three hundred dollars. She wrote them a note."

"So they wouldn't think she was kidnapped or murdered," Elise murmured as she cleaned the last of the chips from her plate. Jasmine appeared to come from a nice home, plenty of food and money. But appearances could be deceiving. A nice home, plenty of food, and money were tangible entities. Emotional abuse knew how to hide in such an environment.

"And then there's David Cagnalia," her father continued. "His mother called me last week. She wants me to let him work here, free, so he'd get some guidance."

"Did you agree?"

"I did. I've always had a soft spot for him and his little brothers. Last year, Jesse gave the younger ones riding lessons. Guess I'd better get them back here, too. It's hard on Margaret Cagnalia, being a single mother of three boys."

"You were a single father of three girls," Elise pointed out.

"Don't be getting all Brady Bunch on me." Her dad shook his toothpick at her.

"And don't call me Alice!" Cook shouted from the kitchen.

"We weren't hurting financially when your mother passed on," her father said. "I was able to hire help when I needed it. Plus, I worked where we lived. I was always available to you girls. If not me, then Cook or Harold," he pointed out, referring to the ranch's long-time foreman.

It was the opening Elise needed to change the subject. "I think I'll head down to the stables. I'd like to see how Pistol's doing, maybe visit a minute or two with Harold." Back when she was in high school, she'd ridden Pistol every day, training for the rodeo. It was strange to think how long she'd been out of the saddle now.

"Harold would love to see you. He's got some ideas about Pistol. You might be interested."

"He's not thinking about retiring and taking Pistol with him, is he?" Elise joked. There were days she'd thought about renting a stall, bringing Pistol to Two Mules. In reality, though, she usually left her trailer at six in the morning and returned at eight at night. She'd be lucky to get one ride in a week. And Pistol, a brown bay with black mane, was lively. High impulsion, her father always said. If Pistol wasn't exercised regularly, he developed an attitude.

"That man will retire after I do," her father said.

A few minutes later, walking down to the stables in a light rain, Elise thought about her father's words. Jacob Hubrecht never spoke about retiring, ever. Now that Jesse, Eva's husband, was helping more, maybe retirement was a possibility. But Jesse Campbell could never love the Lost Dutchman the way Jacob did.

The way Elise did.

She turned around, facing the main house and stared at it, soaking it in, fusing it to her memory.

It was a brown/yellow/orange mixture of color that matched the desert surrounding it and boasted a combination of Santa Fe style and Old West relic. The front porch jutted out and had what looked like tree trunks holding it up. A replica of a Conestoga wagon was to the left of the porch; a modern playground was to the right, complete with a bright blue jungle gym. The rocking chairs on the porch were new. Only the cacti looked exactly the same as they had during her childhood: hot and dry.

Her father had built most of it.

More than once, she'd heard the spiel he gave guests. "She started life as a one-room cabin. Man I bought her from had added two rooms, but neither was up to code. I added electricity, running water and furniture. A few years later, when my wife got pregnant with Eva, she insisted on a bigger house. I completed this beauty when she had my third daughter, Emily."

Elise closed her eyes. She could remember her mother. Naomi Hubrecht had been a slender woman, brown-skinned and strong. Just like Elise. Naomi had ridden many a trail with her husband, and Jacob liked to say she was the only woman who could keep up with him.

"Until you," he'd add, meaning Elise. On that note, Elise turned and continued down the path to the stable. With every step, she saw her past. She'd played amidst the green plants and cacti that flanked the road. Every few yards there was a swing with a canopy. She and Cooper had spent many a night looking at the stars and planning their future. The last thing she passed was a one-room schoolhouse. Judging by the laughter echoing through its walls and to her ears, Patti de la Rosa—the ranch's secretary—was inside, doing crafts with some of the guests' children.

A snort, the horse kind and not the human kind, welcomed her to the stable. Hay crackled a bit under her shoes. Molasses, manure and leather combined together. The sweet smell of home.

Harry Potter, one of the trail horses, was in a stall with a white bandage around his back left ankle. To this day, Elise was amazed that her father let Emily the bookworm name so many of the horses. There had been a moment when Pistol was in danger of being called Wimpy Kid.

Elise smiled. It felt good. As did the entrance to the stable that had at one time been her favorite spot.

Harold Mull looked at her when she entered, half smiled and went back to talking to Harry Potter. "Now, boy, easy does it. You're always getting hurt. Why'd you step into the fence? And, once you stepped in, why did you keep moving until you were hurt? You could have snapped a bone."

"He going to be all right?"

"Harry Potter," Harold predicted, "will be fine." Once Harold finally seemed satisfied with the horse's bandage, he came around the front and exited the stall. Soon, Elise was in a hug that reminded her of the stable: warm, filled with the scent of molasses and leather. Harold's hair was silver, thick, and fit his head like an upside-down bowl. His face was permanently tanned, lined and partly obscured by a full mustache. He looked intimidating and had a gruff attitude to match. In all her days, she'd never seen him hug anyone else. Just her.

The first time it had happened, she'd been eight and in Cinderella's stall crying. She didn't want to be in the main house. Mama wasn't coming home, or so everyone said. The stable was much safer. Nothing had changed down here.

Harold had settled right down beside her and just sat for a while. Then he'd tried singing. There was a reason he was a wrangler and not a country music star. Finally, he'd pulled her in his lap, wrapped his arms around her and rocked. She'd fallen asleep, and he'd carried her home.

They'd been close ever since.

"Pistol needs his exercise," Harold mentioned. "Harry Potter's kept me busy all morning."

Elise looked out the stable door and to her truck. Then she looked out the back of the stable, to the arena, and saw Pistol tied to the fence, waiting his turn. If she went for a ride, she'd wind up staying the night. She'd stayed the night for Eva's wedding. That would be two nights this year. Zero nights for the previous nine.

You're needed in Apache Creek.

"I'll do it. Let me go change clothes and tell Dad I'm staying."

"Good girl," Harold said, in exactly the same tone that he used for the horses.

Twenty minutes later, Elise had on her rain gear and opened the gate to the arena. Pistol stood still for a few moments. Then he started pounding the ground with his left front hoof. His body pressed into the fence as he tried to turn.

"You never forget me. Do you, boy?"

The quick ride turned into three hours. Something about the rainbow, about the small streams forming in the ground, and the way the air smelled, kept her going. When Elise returned to the stable, she removed his tack, groomed him and put him in his stall before heading to the main house just in time for supper.

Eva would be pleased.

Elise, the tension gone from her shoulders, and feeling a good sort of tired, was pleased, too. The warm feeling carried her through supper and through an hour of family time in the Arizona room—where everyone was careful not to make too much of Elise's staying the night.

"Where's Jesse?" Elise asked after Dad finished sharing Emily's latest endeavor. As part of an honor's project, she was working for the Grand Canyon Trust to build homes for Native Americans. She lived farther away from the Lost Dutchman than Elise, but she made it home every few months and every school vacation.

"He's looking into buying a horse from Sunshine Stables over in Queen Creek. The truck broke down near a couple of hours ago. He's getting it fixed. Guess it's pouring there." Dad checked his watch.

From her spot kneeling in front of the loom, Eva said, "I thought he'd be back by now. I've called twice and texted once."

"He's probably by a mountain," Timmy said, sounding just like Jacob, and at six already a well-informed cell phone user. When Elise went to bed just after ten, Jesse still wasn't home. This visit, since the Lost Dutchman was sold out, she was sleeping in Eva's old room. Eva and Jesse were building a home on the west side of the property. Dad had given them the master bed-room until it was finished. He was using the apartment over the stable that had been Jesse and Timmy's when they first moved to the ranch because Eva's bedroom was "too plumb small!" Even smaller was Emily's old bedroom—now converted into a bedroom for Timmy, just as Elise's old room had been turned into an office.

After what felt like just a few hours of sleep, some-one rapped on the door. The sound was soft, polite, at first. Then it got louder, a heavy knocking on the door until she muttered, "Come in."

Timmy opened the door, stuck his head in and then tiptoed over. "It's five in the morning. You're going to miss breakfast."

Elise doubted that's what had him here, waking her up, sounding so much like her dad.

"Thanks." She closed her eyes and turned over.

Timmy didn't leave. Neither did his puppy, Goo-ber, who jumped on the bed and landed next to Elise, his head on the pillow next to hers. Timmy cleared his throat. "Daddy got home an hour ago. He's sleeping. Grandpa says we're full up, and he can't get away. Eva said to ask you."

"Ask me what?" Elise mumbled into her pillow, fig-uring her one attempt at sleeping late had just ended.

"If you'll take me on the gold-panning ride this morning." Then his words came tumbling out. "If you do, I'll never ask you for anything again, and I'll for-give you for not getting me a present last Christmas."

"I got you a present," she protested, still talking to her pillow.

"A whole week after Christmas!"

"I'm going back to Two Mules today, honey. I can't."

In the hallway came Eva's voice, soft but firm. "Can't or won't?"

"I've got things to do." Elise rolled over and stared at the ceiling, wide awake now and trying to think fast.

"More important than your nephew?"

"You know that's not the case."

"You're right." Eva stepped to the door. "What has you the most scared is going on a ride with Cooper. Stepping into your old life. Helping out the family. We've got three horses in a trailer needing to be delivered to him. Guess the ride's full. Say the word and we'll load Pistol as well as Timmy's horse."

"I'm riding Harry Potter. He can really fly," Timmy bragged.

This is why I don't come home.

"I'm not scared of anything." Now, Elise realized, she sounded very much like a middle child who always rose to the occasion when Eva baited her. Timmy's head ping-ponged as he watched the sisters. Goober ignored them all and jumped on Elise's stomach as if saying "You might as well get up." Elise's dogs often did the same thing.

"Prove it," Eva said.

"I don't have to prove anything."

"Tell me, then, one thing you have on your appointment calendar that absolutely has to get done today or the world will end. I'll add you to the church prayer list. You'll receive a hundred cards. Then you'll get phone calls."

Elise threw off the blanket.

"Please, Aunt Elise, I need you to say yes. I want to go."

Apache Creek needs you.

Looked as if she'd be going on a ride.

As the early morning fuzz cleared from her head and she looked out the window at the Arizona sunshine, she could only wonder about the power of prayer.

She knew for a fact that her father had prayed she'd stay the whole weekend.

Funny how this was working out.

Chapter Four

❧

The Last Water parking area already boasted a dozen vehicles. Some with horse trailers, some not. Cooper parked his horse trailer near a corner slot and went around to let PJ out.

The AJ's Outfitters horses and pack mules would be meeting them via Jesse Campbell and the Lost Dutchman Ranch horse trailer, in a few minutes. Jesse would unload the horses while their clients admired the majestic view in front of them and Cooper assigned mounts.

Before Cooper had time to check his watch—something he did more and more now that he was in charge—the horse trailer from the Lost Dutchman Ranch turned onto the dirt road. Cooper watched as it entered the parking area, edged toward the side and then backed into an open area for unloading.

Behind it came Garrett in his old truck with a small horse trailer attached. He'd picked up John Stanford, a teen involved in the Apache Creek Church's youth group who Cooper wished was still Garrett's best friend. John and four of his friends were panning enthusiasts. John had called this morning bemoaning his dad needing the family truck. Cooper had volunteered Garrett to give him a lift.

Garrett parked, stepped out of his truck, and made a face at the Lost Dutchman trailer before coming over to stand next to Cooper and noting, "That's their old one."

They were the first civil words Cooper had gotten from his brother this morning. Eighteen-year-olds didn't take well to being grounded for skipping school.

Cooper frowned. It had only taken the Lost Dutchman truck and trailer but a minute to maneuver into the spot. Usually Jesse was a "slow turn, careful back-up and three attempts to get it perfect" kind of guy. Cooper figured it took more than the year Jesse had been working for the Lost Dutchman to get used to hauling several horses in a gooseneck trailer that made it feel as if you were in charge of a semi.

Elise stepped down from the driver's side. She wore an emerald green button-down shirt that he was certain was Eva's and form-fitting jeans. The boots were hers, well-worn. She gave him a slow wave, said something to the passenger in the truck, and then started to unload the Lost Dutchman's horses as if she'd never been gone.

Garrett muttered something about "needing to get back to the store."

Cooper wondered what was wrong this time. Yesterday, she'd been there to let him know his brother was again causing trouble. Today couldn't possibly be something she wanted to do: not in Apache Creek and certainly not with him.

Elise worked slowly, walking into the trailer, standing at the first horse's shoulder, cueing him to move backward. Giving that horse a gentle pat and a good word once he was out, she moved on to the next. He'd ordered three, knowing he'd get five because Timmy and Jesse would bring their own.

"Where's Jesse?" He kept his voice even. No matter what, she was a potential customer.

"Tire blew out last night and now we've a trailer with a bent axle."

"Everyone all right?"

"Yes, it just meant that he got in very late." Her face was a little pale and her lips were together in a thin line that he recognized as consternation. Nope, she didn't want to be here.

"Somehow," she said, "I became the go-to person to bring Timmy for his ride."

"Aunt Elise is nice." Timmy came around the trailer and hugged her legs even while she tried to lead horses over to the fence and loop their ropes over the top rung. After a moment, she gave up, lifted Timmy into the air, and swung him in a circle. The smile was real. Too bad it didn't go all the way to her eyes.

Usually, Cooper would have motioned Garrett over to help, but Garrett was just as angry with Elise as he was with Cooper. She'd busted him and tattled. That made her public enemy number one.

Elise finally let go of Timmy. The boy pretended to be dizzy and fell to the ground.

"It'll be fine. I still ride on occasion. Your brother coming?" She looked over at Garret.

"No, Garrett's in charge of the store. Come Monday, per your suggestion, he'll be going over to Karl Wilcox's place and repairing the damage done by the truck."

"The other kids, too?"

"Not the girls. They've convinced their parents that

they thought they were only going for a quick ride before school and were terrified when it turned into offroad and extreme trucking."

"And David?"

"I'm not sure. His mom hasn't returned my call."

Honestly, Cooper hoped not. Right now Garrett wasn't strong enough to be a good influence on David. The two just seemed to lead each other into more trouble.

"My dad's been talking to his mother. Looks like he'll be volunteering at our place." She started to walk away, then stilled. Turning around, she looked at Cooper's horse. "You're riding Percy Jackson?"

He'd allowed her little sister to name his horse, all to impress Elise.

"I trained him all through the summer before college. By the time I hit junior year, he turned into the best roping horse I've ever had."

She looked as if she wanted to say something. Instead, she turned to her trailer and started unlatching the doors. Pistol was the last horse Elise led out and clearly unhappy with his position. He bumped into Cooper, a little like Garrett, personally making body contact in a you're-not-my-boss kind of attitude.

"Whoa, boy," Cooper said.

His mother drove up then in their open-air mini-bus with "AJ's Trolley" painted on the side. He'd gotten the logo idea from the Lost Dutchman work trucks. Any advertisement was good advertisement.

Other than his mother, the only female on board was a curly-haired redhead, who smacked gum and had a forty-five-year-old body wedged into a twenty-five-year-old's outfit.

The hair wasn't real, either.

When Cooper had signed her up over the phone, she claimed she could ride. Soon they'd find out if she was telling the truth.

The teens were off the bus in a shot. Others moved more slowly, sipping the last of their coffee; some were taking pictures and talking excitedly. Taking a breath, Cooper said, "Now that the horses are ready, I'll match you to a mount and we'll get going."

"I wouldn't mind that one," the redhead said, looking at Pistol.

"He belongs to the wrangler from the Lost Dutchman," Cooper said without hesitating. Elise neither smiled nor frowned at her description; she just kept working.

He put the redhead on a speckled gray mare.

"Flea-bitten," the redhead complained. Meaning, either the woman was knowledgable about horses or she didn't mind being derogatory without knowing what she was talking about.

Elise spoke up. "He's part Arabian and offers a good seat."

The woman nudged the horse into a slow walk, then into a trot, making it look easy.

"You've got a lot of teenagers," Elise said in a low voice to Cooper. "Is that typical?"

"They go to my church. We've formed a sort of gold-panning club."

"Garrett a member?"

Cooper checked to see what his brother was doing. Garrett, however, was nowhere about. "No, I wish he were." Almost for emphasis, Cooper looked at his watch. "It's time to go."

The driver's door to the AJ's Outfitters bus slowly opened and Karen Smith gingerly stepped out. Another not-so-good day. He kept thinking his mom would rebound, soon, but Dad's death had changed her. "Elise Hubrecht! Is that you?"

She left the door open. She usually hurried back to the store, especially if Garrett was in charge. Instead, now she somewhat limped across the lot and took Elise into her arms. "We have missed you. If I'd known you were along for the ride, I'd have saddled up to come, too."

Leaving Garrett alone to manage the store. Cooper didn't think so. "Mom, Elise is in town for the weekend."

"I heard you might be taking a job at the high school," Karen said.

"Slim possibility."

Cooper raised an eyebrow. He'd heard she'd be out of work in a week and had plenty of bills to cover.

"I need some help here," someone called. At first Cooper attributed the high-pitched voice to the redhead, but instead it was a middle-aged man who was tagging along with a younger man. Both looked to be businessmen. They were probably on a quest to escape their overburdened desks.

Cooper had to hurry because Timmy was heading their way, and in Cooper's experience, businessmen usually didn't take kindly to six-year-olds telling them what to do, especially if the six-year-old was better at it than they were.

"So, how'd you wind up going on this ride?" he heard his mother ask from behind him.

Cooper helped the businessman while Elise explained about her brother-in-law's misadventures. "He's still asleep. Not to mention, he managed to cut up his hand trying to get the spare on."

"We think the world of Jesse. He's been talking to our youth about his experience going to prison—how he found faith while he was inside and turned his life around, taking the job at Lost Dutchman when he got out and committing to his fresh start. I think the single girls still get a kick out of him. They, whether teen or not, show up every time to hear his message about avoiding trouble, rising above your raising, and forgiving self. I just wish more listened."

"Jesse's spoken at the high school in Two Mules, too."

Cooper wasn't surprised.

"He's a blessing," Karen said. "The kids admire him, but Garrett's not quite getting the message. He summed it up one night with an 'I don't like when people tell me not to do what they did. Obviously, to them, at one time, it looked like a whole lotta fun. I want to make my own mistakes.'"

"Did you point out that Jesse had to spend five years in prison paying for his mistakes?"

"Yes, but it didn't seem to impress Garrett. His 'not gonna happen to me' stance remained firm." Karen looked over at the dust blowing up from the road as Garrett drove away. "Thank you for corralling him yesterday morning. I don't know what's gotten into him. We all miss his dad, but this behavior…"

Looking over at Elise as she leaned in to hear his mother's words, Cooper wondered if she could help. If she was willing to stay. Problem was, she ran when the going got tough. Always had. At first, it had been on Pistol's back and through Lost Dutchman property, never far. Then, when everyone needed her, when *he* needed her, she'd run away to the big city, never planning to return.

Cooper didn't dare trust Garrett to a woman who couldn't stay. Not so close to their father's departure.

With that thought, he stepped away from the young businessman he'd just shown how to mount. Looked as if the redhead wasn't the one he needed to worry about, so he decided to treat her just like everyone else; except, he didn't need to spend three minutes telling her what kind of horse she was on.

He waved goodbye to his mother and then swung onto the back of Percy Jackson and led the pack. The redhead, whose name turned out to be Jilly Greenhouse, fell in love with the speckled gray ten minutes out.

"This is great."

Cooper soon realized that if Jilly just knew when to stop talking, she'd be perfect on the trail. She took Timmy under her wing. He was the only other person chewing gum. Strange thing to bond over, but friendships had been formed by less.

The horses knew their way, so Cooper dropped back, checking on his charges. The two businessmen were from New York. It turned out they were father and son. The father grew up riding and now regretted not giving his son the same upbringing. The son looked as if he'd rather be anywhere but here. Jilly scooted her horse over to the young businessman and soon her chattering distracted him.

As if knowing her job, Elise took the end. Only the pack mules were behind her, the panning equipment they carried making its presence known with every step. The five teenagers were in front of her. Judging by their backward glances, they wished she were in front of them.

They were the same age, Cooper and Elise, both of them twenty-eight. She didn't look it. She still looked the same as she did the last time he kissed her.

When everyone seemed comfortable, Cooper launched into his desert drawl. "We're heading up a trail on the Superstition Mountains. You can also consider this the Tonto National Forest. No matter, this is wilderness. Today is approximately sixty-eight degrees. We sun-dwellers call this winter."

The businessmen chuckled appreciatively. One of the teenagers offered Elise his jacket and told her she rode a horse well. Cooper realized that when he'd been doing introductions, she'd been off doing something to one of the horses. The kid would be all kinds of embarrassed when he found out that Elise was Jacob Hubrecht's middle daughter, the one with all the rodeo trophies.

Hiding a smile, Cooper continued his monologue. "We'll be heading to an area known for after-rain puddles and streams. Hopefully, the rain has moved some gold out of caves and down the side. On a good day, you can make up to fifty dollars."

"And on a bad day?" Jilly asked.

"You'll have fifty insect bites."

He earned a few chuckles before he continued, "We'll be riding amidst boulders and both saguaro and barrel cactus."

Two riders coming down the trail stopped and cautioned Cooper about a bobcat they'd seen a short way up.

About the time Cooper was going to mention the

jumping-cholla cacti, Timmy squealed, like only a six-year-old could do. "Aunt Elise, there's something sticking me, by my ankle."

"The dreaded teddy bear cholla." Elise easily slid from Pistol and went to the boy, adding, "Nothing cuddly about it." In a few moments, she'd taken her pocket knife, removed the culprit before its hollow stems could do much damage, and had Timmy calm and ready to move forward, although now on the lookout for pods that would aim their painful oval balls of needles at him.

"Pretty good." Jilly nodded her approval. "I always carry a comb with me. Think it's easier to use."

"Aunt Elise?"

Cooper turned back to the riders. Timmy looked eager to return to the trail, not so the five teenagers. They were looking at Elise. A nudge of jealousy tapped Cooper on the shoulder. He ignored it.

"Aunt Elise would be me." Elise smiled at the teenager who just twenty minutes ago had offered her his jacket.

He slowed his horse so he could ride close to her. "You're Cooper's old girlfriend?"

"I'm not old," she said easily.

"You won the Arizona High School State Rodeo Finals and the National High School Rodeo Finals."

She changed her mind. "I am old. That was a long time ago. I'm just here today riding with my nephew."

"What's the difference between cholla and cactus?"

"Cholla is just a type of cactus," Timmy said.

"There's also the Christmas cholla," Cooper said, watching as Elise flicked her hair and remounted. The teenage boys, especially John Stanford—an eighteen-year-old, someday headed for law school but first gonna get rich by discovering gold—continued to watch her. Everyone else seemed enraptured by the stark beauty of the Arizona desert.

Cooper knew stark beauty when he saw it. Today it wasn't evident in the landscape but in Elise. He forgot himself for a moment and studied her when he should have kept his eye on where he was going. He nearly rode right into a jumping-cactus bush and a pod attached itself to his leg. Its spikes went right through his jeans and what felt like a dozen needles quickly penetrated.

"We're stopping," he ground out.

He quickly dismounted and pulled his jean away from his leg. Each time a spike separated from his flesh, two others seem to find a fresh target in the same spot. Before he could do more than mutter "I've had better days" both Elise and Jilly were by his side.

"Stop hopping around," Elise advised. "You're making it worse." As if to prove her point, another pod actually landed on his boot and he could feel the spikes through the leather.

"Plus, you'll knock us into the cactus," Jilly added.

Like a calf, they had him down on the ground, leg up, in just under five seconds.

"You're thorough," Jilly said. "I don't think there's going to be an inch of your left leg that doesn't have red marks."

"Are you going to take his pants off?" John asked.

"Nothing I haven't seen," said Jilly. "I'm a nurse."

Elise promptly dropped the leg she was holding, and Cooper yelped as he felt the spikes break through his jeans and latch on again. "You know," she said, almost casually, "the Indians used these as weapons. They were quite effective." For a moment, the old Elise stood over him, teasing, funny, full of life.

But the old Elise wouldn't have let Jilly finish removing the spikes. She'd have pitched in, too.

Well, at least this time, the wound Elise dealt wasn't to the heart.

Elise didn't allow herself to laugh. Really, it wasn't funny but the teenagers were still grinning, and Cooper took it in good spirits. He mounted his horse with a stoic grimace, even though Elise knew it had to hurt. Timmy eyed the jumping-cholla plant with a new respect. "I've never seen Cooper look mad," he shared.

Great, first time hanging with her ex-boyfriend in a decade and she'd managed to make his day. And not in a good way. She should have helped remove the pods. She'd done it plenty of times for him when they were younger.

Well, best thing to do was stay clear of him for the rest of the trip. Elise took Pistol down to a slow walk. It allowed her to keep track of everyone, especially Timmy. This was the first time she'd gone anywhere, just the two of them.

Looking around, she found Timmy riding by one of the teenagers and laughing. What a difference a year made. Before Timmy's father had gotten out of jail, Jesse hadn't even known he had a son. The boy had lived with his mother, a drug addict, up until shortly before Jesse's release. When he was passed over to Jesse on the day of his release, Timmy had been in bad shape—underweight, under-socialized and too terrified of the world around him to even speak.

In just a year, Timmy had gone from a mute five-year-old who preferred hiding under a table to an adventurous six-year-old who could banter and sit a horse. It reminded Elise how much of a difference a committed, determined adult could make in the life of a child.

The teens were a happy bunch, joking with each other with an ease born of a lifetime of friendship. Elise urged her horse up next to the one who'd singled her out the most.

"So, does Garrett ever come on these rides?"

"He used to," the teenager said, "back when his dad was alive. I don't think he's come since then." After a little hesitation, he added, "He hangs with a different crowd."

No surprise.

"What's your name?"

"John Stanford."

Stanford, not a name she remembered. "You attend Apache Creek High School?"

He grinned, "It's my senior year. I'll be off to Arizona State University come August."

"Are you friends with Jasmine Taylor?"

The open, friendly look disappeared. Elise recognized the shut-down mechanism used by any youth when an adult got too nosey. She'd just gone from being a cute rodeo champion to being an untrustworthy adult with a mission. In Elise's experience, honesty was always the best policy.

"I was at the high school yesterday. They offered me a job. I'm a social worker. Right now, I work in Two Mules, Arizona, mostly with teens."

A little of the distrust ebbed away. "I've never heard of Two Mules."

"It's on a reservation a few hours from here, near the New Mexico border."

"You still ride and compete?"

"I don't compete, but I still ride. I have a rancher friend who lends me a horse any time I want it." She'd helped his daughter, an unwed mother, make goals and keep them. First, how to care for her newborn. Next, returning to school. Finally, naming the father and going after support. It had been a year-long venture, but it paid off substantial dividends. Not only had the girl gotten her life together, but her father had been grateful enough to agree to partner with Elise on her pet project of getting the Two Mules teens on horses.

"I've been trying to start a program in Two Mules where teens have a place to go after school," she said, "working with horses and maybe even competing."

"We ride some in Cooper's backyard arena. He's taught us how to rope. Not that we're any good. It's fun. I wish your dad still had a program at the high school. I'd have joined. Maybe while you're here, you can show us a few things."

She started to use the word "old" again but stopped. There were women older than she who were All American Quarter Horse Congress Barrel Racing Sweepstakes champions. She watched the competitions, sometimes turning the television or computer screen off because of a longing she no longer wanted to have.

"No, I've changed my focus."

"Why?"

No way was she going to get into a discussion about why with a high school senior, one who was the very age Elise had been when Cindy died.

"Sometimes you make choices in your life that are

more for the good of others than for yourself," Elise finally offered.

John didn't look too impressed.

"You here to help Garrett?" he asked.

"Does Garrett need help?"

John nodded. With that, he clicked his tongue and nudged his horse forward. Only then did Elise notice that the horses were slowing down and that Cooper had already dismounted and was staring at her.

He used to read lips pretty good. At least, her lips.

The five teens, along with Elise, Timmy and Jilly, all dismounted and took care of their horses without instruction. The older businessman watched and soon followed the others' example. The younger man, though, had clearly had enough of his horse. Elise noted a tiny bit of fear in the man's eyes; Cooper apparently saw it, too, and took over.

Looking around at the mounds of dirt Elise tried to remember if she'd been to this location before. It didn't look familiar, but then back when she and Cooper were an item, they didn't do excursions with the public. They'd explored parts of the Superstition that few ventured to.

"You ever see a rattlesnake?" the young businessman asked.

"Not in the winter," Cooper replied.

"Does Arizona have a winter?"

Elise said soothingly, "Yes, and this is it. Don't worry."

When everyone was ready, Cooper opened up the packs he'd slung on the mules and started handing out supplies. AJ's had come a long way in the ten years she'd been gone. The water bottles had "AJ's Outfitters" as the label. There was even a thin plastic lunchbox bearing the logo and filled with a sandwich, chips, apples and a water bottle.

"The best time to pan," Cooper said, "is in winter. That's what we'll be working with today. Because this is wilderness, we can't take dirt home with us."

The young businessman rolled his eyes as if saying "Who'd want to?"

Elise noted Timmy's eyes go wide with excitement. He pulled a pan from his saddlebag and waited. Soon Cooper had the teenagers and Jilly sitting on flat rocks in front of a small stream. Elise accepted a pan and soon was kneeling next to Timmy, with pan in the stream and then busy shaking the dirt and mud out.

"Don't be afraid to dig in," Cooper advised. "You need the gravel loosened up. Use your water. With your fingers, get the bigger pebbles out. Keep adding water— you want to thoroughly wash your findings." Bending down next to Timmy, he gently put his hands over the boy's. "You don't want to tip so much that you lose your gravel. You want to keep what you brought up the first time. Your job is to shake back and forth until the gold sinks to the bottom."

"You really think there's gold in my pan?" Timmy didn't slow down much, even with Cooper trying to taper his movements.

"I think there's always the possibility."

"You ever find gold?" the younger businessman asked.

"Yes."

It was enough to convince everyone to get back to work. Jilly said something about recently buying property in Apache Creek and needing the money.

"How much could I earn today?" Timmy asked.

"Very few people find gold their first time out," Cooper advised.

"And probably not from a claim visited as often as this one," the older businessman added.

"That true?" Timmy's movements slowed. Muddy water tipped over his hands and some gravel spilled out before Cooper could stop it. Elise held her pan still. She'd been shaking back and forth, carefully adding clean water to the muddy, flicking out pieces of stone that didn't belong.

"I keep coming up here because I believe," Cooper said.

It was good enough for Timmy. "Like Santa," he breathed. Elise nodded. No way would she hinder a dream. Both of them got back to business.

Cooper went from person to person until all were comfortable. Then he got out his pan, one Elise recognized as handed down from his father, and started panning. His movements were quick and sure. Like he was. He'd taught her to pan, sidled up beside her, his strong hands on hers.

Cindy had come a time or two, never really wanting to get dirty but never wanting to be left out. She'd usually messed with her phone instead of the dirt.

Elise would have dug all the way to China if it meant staying next to him with his arms around her.

As if sensing her thoughts, he moved away from her and Timmy, and joined the two businessmen. Elise was surprised at how annoyed she felt.

She'd liked him next to her.

Even after all this time.

Easily, he started telling the history of the area. "The

Native Americans didn't much like this mountain. They believed that evil people were punished by being turned into stone and stuck forever at the top, forced to watch as the good people lived below."

"Kind of a new twist on Lot's wife being turned into a pillar of salt?" John said. Elise got the impression he'd heard the spiel a dozen times and knew right when to heckle.

"I thought it was a pillow of salt," Timmy said. "I even drew it in Bible class one day."

To Elise's surprise, it was the businessman who answered. "That event took place near the Dead Sea. If you took a sip out of water in your pan, young man, you'd spit it out. Too muddy. If you were near the Dead Sea and took a drink, you'd spit it out, too, because of the salt."

Timmy looked at the water in his pan as if considering.

"What's cool about the Dead Sea is because of all the minerals and such in the water, sometimes near the shore will come a spout. Do you know what a spout is?"

Timmy shook his head. The teens and Jilly nodded. The young businessman continued, for the first time showing a personality. "You know how a whale will spout water?" After Timmy's nod, he went on. "Well, the water of the Dead Sea is also under the shore a bit. And, sometimes the water spouts out of the beach, like water comes out of a whale's spout. But because of the salt and minerals instead of coming down like water from a fountain, it comes down and forms a lump, which grows and grows each time the water spouts."

The older businessman nodded. "It stays, like a rock

formation, mostly made out of salt and sometimes called a pillar of salt."

They'd lost Timmy, but the teens looked amazed.

"I'm going there some day," Jilly said.

"I'll show you some pictures on the internet when we get home," Elise promised Timmy.

"I'm glad you're home." He hugged her, spilling muddy water and gravel on her leg.

She looked down at Cooper, expecting to hear a "Me, too," but instead he continued, "Ol' Lot's wife," Cooper said, "looked back on a town not worth noticing."

"She wasn't bad, though," Timmy pointed out.

"No," the older businessman said. "She just didn't like change. She wasn't brave."

"It takes someone brave to leave what they know and make a new life," his son added.

"And it takes someone brave to come home when they're needed." Timmy was referring to the gold-panning trip and her taking him.

She was thinking about Jasmine Taylor, the runaway, and David Cagnalia, who'd robbed a convenience store and now ran around with Garrett Smith.

She should also be thinking about Tammi White-wheather and Clint Ouray, two teens in Two Mules who needed her. Tammi was expecting her second child and was addicted to meth. Clint was skipping school and had no plans, not a one, for the future. His only love was video games.

And although she shouldn't be, she was thinking about Cooper.

Elise went back to panning and wished there were two of her.

It wasn't the first time she'd made such a wish. Used to be, instead of wishes, she prayed. So far, she didn't see much in the way of fruition from either. And, working in Two Mules, making a difference with the kids, was exhausting—not just to her body but to her spirit. More so than Elise liked to admit.

But today wasn't the time to dwell on hardships. Timmy had unearthed a flake on the side of a rock wall that looked like something. Elise thought possibly fool's gold, but it didn't matter to the boy. Pretty soon, she was crawling alongside him, switching from panning for gold to rock climbing. Funny how a day spent panning, getting dirty, joking with mostly strangers, plus eating sandwiches, chips and an apple with only water to wash them down could take the stress right out of a person. By the time Cooper checked his watch and said it was time to go, she was sorry to have the day end. The trek down the mountain to the parking area went too quickly.

She even laughed when Cooper gave her a dirty look where the jumping cholla waited. Timmy was convinced that he'd both panned gold as well as discovered a cache of rocks that he declared were "rare."

Once back at the parking lot where Garrett was waiting, she, Garrett and Cooper took care of the horses and mules. Once she had the ones from the Lost Dutchman loaded, she and Timmy headed for home. They had barely pulled into the parking area in front of the stable before Timmy jumped out of the truck, the horses forgotten, and went to his dad who was sure to appreciate the precious "gems" more than Elise.

"How'd it go?" Her father came from the back barn

as Elise put down the back of the trailer and stood talking to the first horse she wanted to back out.

"We went to a different area than Cooper used to take me to."

"He's put some time and ideas into the business. Once his dad took sick, Cooper came home to take over the guide portion of the operation—and then, gradually, everything else, too. He's got a good head for business. You know that rodeo arena he has in the backyard?"

She knew it well.

"He's been having a few events. Small, but I know he's brought in some extra money. His mom has always been one of the best cooks in town. People come just to buy her pies."

"When was the last time he rodeoed? Do you know?"

"Not since he's been back. I'm thinking his little brother's keeping him too busy for much else other than family and work."

That didn't sound like the fun-loving, adventurous boy she remembered. But ten years was plenty of time for a person to change. And that just made her heart ache again when she thought of Cindy—her best friend who'd never get the chance to grow into the woman she could have been. "Dad, I don't think I can come home. Everything here reminds me of Cindy. I can see her standing in the barn, right here, waiting for me and complaining about how much time I spent with the horses."

Her dad helped as she cared for the horses. "You're always going to miss her," he said simply. "But missing her doesn't always have to hurt. Coming home, facing those memories—maybe that's just what you need to do to find some peace."

Her father continued, "For what time she had on this earth, you were a good friend. Sometimes that has to be enough."

Elise wished that were true. All she could ever think, when it came to Cindy, was if she'd taken the time to check her phone, she'd have seen Cindy's last text. She'd have known that Cindy's boyfriend had been drinking, and that she wanted a safe ride home. A ride that Elise should have given her. And nothing she did, then or now, could change the fact that she hadn't.

Because she didn't, Cindy died.

And something inside Elise had died, too.

Chapter Five

AJ's Outfitters closed its doors at six on Saturday evening. In the three hours since he'd returned from the panning outing, Cooper had been playing catch-up. Maybe because Garrett was afraid of getting in more trouble, he'd not left the place in a mess. They'd also had a few good sales.

Cooper flipped the sign to Closed: Open Again Monday, locked the door behind him and stepped down the walkway. His truck, bright red and fairly new, waited for him. Like him, it was alone in the parking lot.

Looking down the dirt road, he could see distant lights. AJ's was in town, but on a short side road that had no other businesses. It backed up to a wilderness area where he could take Percy Jackson and ride for miles. In the night's silence, he could hear faint laughter coming from a restaurant on the corner before their road. Apache Creek was a rustic, Western, small town, but there was a peacefulness to it that he loved. Now that he'd been back a whole year, gotten involved with the church youth group and his old friends, there was no other place he wanted to settle in.

He pulled out his phone and checked for messages. He had two, both related to work.

For the last few months, he'd been so busy that he'd not noticed how alone he felt. Today, panning for gold with Elise had reminded him of how it felt to look down the way and see something, someone, who belonged to him, belonged to his heart.

Not that Elise belonged to him in any way—not anymore. That warmly possessive feeling was a remnant of the past, just a memory stirred up by seeing her familiar face in that very familiar setting. But it reminded him of how nice it had been, back when they were just kids, to have someone to love. And how much he missed having someone to fill that hole in his life now.

He'd not dated since returning home. He'd arrived exactly one year and two days ago when he was told that his father had collapsed behind the counter. A week later, he'd been standing in the exact same space, trying to give advice on setting up a sluice box, when the phone rang. It was his mother calling from Phoenix to say Mitch Smith wouldn't be coming back to work. Just over two months later, Cooper's had dad passed away.

At the funeral, he'd sat next to his little brother and watched as his mother spoke to family members and friends. He'd nodded at people, tried to speak when they came over to tell him how sorry they were, but mostly he'd been numb. Before his dad's collapse, Cooper had been two years into a career in Moab, Utah. Working at a helium plant wasn't his dream job, but it was pretty close. His work ethic—long hours and always on time—quickly moved him up the ladder. The pay was good since it was a Fortune 500 company, the conditions were good since it wasn't desk work, and best of all, Moab had a thriving outdoor community. He'd left the world of horses behind and got involved in mountain biking, hiking and rafting.

When the casseroles stopped and his mother's tears went from a torrent to a trickle, they went through his father's desk. Mitch had done right by his family. They had enough in the bank for his mother to live comfortably the rest of her life. They could sell the house, the horses, the business and…

Right now, the business was running in the black, but they didn't have as much of a cushion as Cooper would like. However, with the side mining excursion and establishing a strong online presence, eventually he might make more than he had at his Moab job. It would also put him where he could take care of his mother. Those had been his first two thoughts. Then he'd realized he couldn't get rid of AJ's so easily. He loved the store. But the biggest realization had been that his mother wasn't the one who needed him most.

His little brother was.

And so he didn't sell the horses, or the house, or the business. At twenty-eight years of age, he was taking care of and paying the bills for a redbrick ranch-style home his parents had had custom-built twenty years ago on the outskirts of town.

It was a twenty-minute ride from AJ's Outfitters.

"I saved supper," his mother said when he shook off his jacket and settled down on the couch. "Noodle soup."

Plenty of it, too, Cooper saw. "Garrett not eating?" He hoped.

"No, I mean yes. He ate two helpings." She nodded towards the open box of crackers on the counter.

"You didn't eat, Mom?"

He waited for the "I'm not hungry" and "I'll eat later" or "I'm cutting back." For the last few months, his mother hadn't been hungry, hadn't eaten later. When she didn't say anything, he decided to be proactive.

Taking two bowls from the cabinet, he ladled soup for both him and his mother. He'd sit down across from her, get her talking, and make sure she'd eat. At least being grounded hadn't changed Garrett's appetite. There were maybe three cracker crumbs left.

"That boy…" His mother shook her head while taking the plate Cooper offered.

From down the hallway he could hear music coming from Garrett's room. No doubt his brother was playing video games. Maybe Cooper should have taken those away, too, but the idea of his brother stuck at home with nothing to do was too much to bear.

"It was nice seeing Elise. She looks the same."

Cooper nodded. Actually, she looked better except for the eyes. Her eyes now had a haunted look that hadn't been there before. It made him want to take her in his arms, offer his protection.

Not his love. Been there, done that, been rejected.

"Think she might take the job?"

"Soup's good, Mom. Why don't you take a bite?"

She did, a tiny one, and then looked at him expectantly.

"I don't think she wants to come back to Apache Creek."

"We were all hurting when Cindy Hamm died in that awful crash, but Cindy wouldn't want Elise to still be broken up about it. If she'd only talk to Mike, give up the burden."

"Everyone deals with loss differently." He shook a fork at her. "Some people stop eating."

She took another bite of food. "My loss of appetite is because I'm not hungry. That's it."

"Want me to leave you alone?"

She nodded.

"Then go to the doctor on Monday. Get a check-up."

"Why? I'm fine. You get older, things change, I just don't eat as much." With that, she took her plate to the sink, scraped most of the food into the garbage disposal and headed to her bedroom saying, "I think I'll lie down."

Another Saturday night to spend either balancing the books, bothering Garrett, or in front of the TV.

Fun.

Cooper headed outside, turned on the floodlights, and grabbed his nylon lariat. There were no longhorns, no one to drive the quad and pull the roping dummy, and no second person for his team.

He worked alone.

Just like he had in college and a few years after when he'd been rodeoing as a breakaway roper. After an hour of catching what he aimed for, Cooper was ready for bed and thinking that maybe he needed to buy a few longhorns, just to keep handy in case things changed.

Sunday morning, the whole Smith clan headed for his mother's Taurus. Garrett sat sullen in the back. Cooper drove. His mom leaned back in the passenger seat, pensive and withdrawn. Garrett's attitude was no surprise, but Cooper wished he knew what was going on with his mom.

"Want to go to Miner's Lamp for lunch?" he suggested.

"No," Garrett said.

His mother offered a half-hearted, "Maybe."

"Look!" Garrett actually sounded excited about something. Cooper took his foot off the gas, slowed and glanced over to see what his brother was pointing at.

It was Elise, on Pistol. She wore the white cowboy hat he remembered well. Her hair flowed out behind her as she navigated the trail behind Apache Creek park. She and the horse were fluid, one movement: graceful, elegant, breathtaking.

It didn't escape Cooper's notice that she turned and was soon riding away from him.

Elise returned to Two Mules as the sun went down on Sunday. Like Apache Creek it had a main street that dated back to the eighteen hundreds. But while Apache Creek had grown and flourished, Two Mules was struggling to hold itself together. Families on the rez could trace their roots and the tree didn't go far. Many of the children were leaving, following jobs and/or education. The recently completed pipeline had been a boost in the economy, but now that it was done, Two Mules was pretty much a remnant of a long-ago era. One without a McDonalds or Walmart. Unfortunately, it wasn't post-card-pretty, either. There were no Victorian houses, and if there'd ever been white picket fences, they were brown and decaying now.

Her phone pinged. Elise checked the screen. A late-night phone call from her sister Emily was not what she needed. Still, Elise didn't interrupt the prerequi-site greeting and weather info exchange before asking the obvious.

"Did Eva tell you to call me?" Elise knew her older

sister too well. If something was wrong, Eva wanted to fix it and believed that the best remedy was a sister Band-Aid.

"She said you might take a job in Apache Creek and that you barely smiled the whole weekend. Is the thought of returning home that bad?"

Elise thought back. On a regular daily basis, she didn't usually feel too melancholy over Cindy's absence. All the years of learning about counseling, doing the counseling, being counseled, must have finally paid off. But that was only true when she was away from home. If Elise didn't spend time in Apache Creek, she could almost imagine that Cindy was still alive. Going back, even for a short time, had brought all that pain back to the surface. And yet—

"I actually had a pretty good time," Elise admitted, because she had enjoyed spending time with her family, and riding again. "I helped out at the ranch and even took Timmy gold-panning."

"With Cooper," Emily filled in what Elise left out.

"He's doing well and seems to enjoy running his dad's business." Quickly Elise filled Emily in on the adventures of Cooper's little brother.

"Does it scare you, the thought of helping people who are basically an extension of our family?" Emily asked.

Elise opened her mouth, then closed it again. Emily was an old soul who had always been way too wise for her years. She was the keeper of history.

And used it as a weapon.

"Maybe," Elise admitted. "But truly the biggest hindrance is I'm needed in both places and I'm just starting to make a difference here."

Emily accepted the response with half-hearted agreement. For the next few minutes, they talked about Emily's current job working for the Utah Department of History and Arts. She was all aglow about a Ute visual art exhibit going on display near Salt Lake City.

Elise felt better after the call ended. No matter what life threw at her, she had a dad and two sisters to flank her, different though they may be.

To Elise's surprise, she fell right to sleep that night, not allowing herself to fret over her uncertain future.

Her good mood dimmed some as she rolled out of bed Monday morning and got ready for her day. She had a full schedule: five home visits and two office. Then there'd be paperwork.

Last night's dream stayed with her as she ate breakfast and got dressed. She'd thought Cooper's image banished, but—probably because of Saturday's ride—he was back in her thoughts and knocking for entry.

No, not a good idea, better to think about work.

Because none of her caseload visits today were to new clients, she wore jeans and a T-shirt. Two Mules was not a fancy town. Contrary to what some of her more stoic professors had taught, here she was more likely to be received if she dressed casually rather than in a dark blue suit and white blouse.

T-shirts were much more effective. It had been a rodeo T-shirt that helped her connect with seventeen-year-old Gina Morningdove's father, Randall, just a few months ago. He'd been ready to toss his pregnant daughter out, at best; hunt down the baby's father and shoot him, at worst. By the end of that visit, she and Randall were both riding horses down the road in front of his house and discussing who was the greatest rodeoer ever: Ty Murray or Trevor Brazile. They followed that hot topic with prenatal care for Gina. Gina had no mothers or aunts, so Dad needed to be aware.

Not every visit was quite so successful.

Her first visit today had to do with truancy. She doubted she'd make much headway. What she really needed was someone at the school to take up her cause, find a reason besides learning for kids to get together.

"What I should have majored in," she muttered to herself as she shut the door to her trailer behind her and locked the door, "was Non-Profit Leadership and Management." Then she could get programs in the school and be tangibly proactive instead of helplessly retroactive.

With that thought in mind, she walked down the sidewalk and climbed into her ancient, hand-me-down-but-paid-for truck.

Maybe if Clint Ouray had a horse, where he'd be outside smelling the sunshine and getting exercise, she could get him away from his video games and remembering to live! She saw potential buried in his eyes— potential that would be lost if he kept skipping school. He just needed something to spark it.

She'd never skipped school. Her dad would have killed her.

Hah, and she really should remind Cooper that he had skipped school, so he shouldn't get too upset with Garrett.

That thought took her back to last night's dream. Cooper had been leaning against the fence while she rode Pistol. Even in the dream, Elisa had been bothered because he was trying to make her laugh, and she didn't want to. He didn't even have his horse. Then he stopped shouting encouragements. He merely watched, his loopy smile gone. In the dream, Elise wanted to ride Pistol over to him and ask what was wrong. But the crazy horse would only ride in circles, and Elise held on, wanting the ride to end, but not knowing how to pull on the reins.

She had the feeling that if she'd managed to dismount, her knees would have collapsed and she'd not have been able to crawl to either the main house or to Cooper. She'd have stayed in the practice arena. Alone.

Turning the ignition switch to the royal blue two-fifty Ford truck that had the Lost Dutchman's logo—now too faded to read—on the door, she hit the gas and headed to work. Behind her was the dirt lot, the slightly off-balance purple-and-beige mobile home she'd lived in for the past four years, along with her two dogs Raven and Gray Fox. She wished they were in the cab with her. They'd distract her from the still-clinging dream that silently whispered, "Time to go home."

Luckily, Elise didn't put too much stock in dreams. They were what they were…a bundle of whatever was on one's mind.

And Cooper was definitely on her mind. Maybe it was because they hadn't really had closure. Before Cindy's death, they'd had their lives charted out together: joint scholarships as a rodeo team, and joined hearts from a teenage romance still going strong. But after Cindy's funeral, she'd told him she couldn't be with him anymore. At eighteen, she'd changed her way of life. She'd stopped focusing on self and started focusing on others.

It hadn't been easy. For the first two years of university, she'd existed in a vacuum—attending classes, doing homework, never straying too far from her little apartment. She'd had little interest in socializing, and her dating life had been nonexistent. Her junior and senior year, she'd been too busy to spend time thinking of the past much. Her senior year, she'd spent a month in a small town in Mexico helping to rebuild it after a tornado destroyed everything. Never before had she realized the luxury she'd grown up in. She'd had her own room, her own horse and never doubted that the next meal would appear on the table. She came back changed, knowing that she could and would help. In Apache Creek, she'd not been there for Cindy Hamm. In Two Mules, she was there for Gina Morningdove, Tammi Whitefeather and Clint Ouray.

It took her only five minutes to drive to work. Her office was in a yellow pre-fab building that was nice compared to the old and faded businesses flanking it. Most of them had For Sale signs hanging on smudged glass. The parking lot was gravel and three trees fought for survival in the front. Only one was winning. Elise hurried up the wheelchair ramp entrance because the stairs were broken. Air-conditioning welcomed her, and she paused a moment, trying to get her bearings.

"You've had two phone calls," Rachel Nez said, after Elise closed the door behind her.

All told, the Division of Social Services was divided into four departments—family, child care, adult and violence prevention—and had five employees. Rachel was full-blooded Hopi and had managed the office for seventeen years.

"Emergencies?" Probably not. Elise was assistant to the woman who ran the child-care department. Tina Romaro was a twenty-year employee, did a good job, but kept herself distant from those she served and from

Elise. She knew how to leave work at work. Even after four years, Tina considered Elise still in training. And, as Elise was just twenty-eight, the others tended to try to protect her. Mostly because she never emotionally clocked out.

"The Sakiestewas didn't show up for counseling," Rachel reported.

"Not surprising," Elisa said. "The husband agreed to it because he was scared. The wife agreed to it because the husband did. Neither think they need it." For the children's sake, Elise would make a couple of phone calls.

"Then Tammi Whitefeather's sister called. Tammi's in the hospital over in Globe. Wynita said there's nothing to worry about."

Nothing to worry about? Hah. Elise pulled her cell phone from her purse and checked messages. She had nothing from Tammi or Wynita, which told her something was going on. Tammi called whenever she needed outside help caring for her two-year-old. A single mother at fifteen, now about to be one again at seventeen, Tammi kept making one bad choice after another. Elise wanted to cry. Every time she thought Tammi was listening to the advice, trying to better herself, the teenager turned around and did something foolish.

Elise had little doubt as to why Tammi was in the hospital. If they kept her a few days, she'd sober up. If they didn't, she'd be out on the town tonight, leaving her daughter with whoever agreed to watch her.

It took only a moment to punch in first Tammi's and then Wynita's phone numbers. Neither girl answered. The downside to smartphones was they announced who was calling. Obviously Tammi didn't want to hear Elise scold. Elise sent a text to Wynita promising to stop by today.

A small desk behind a partition made up Elise's work station. As she sat down, she heard the other social workers checking in for the day. Although field visits were the priority, much of their time was spent with paperwork and telephone calls. Speaking of time, there was never enough. Elise's day had just gotten longer because field visit number five was all the way in Globe.

She got in her truck and started driving, only making it a few miles before her cell sounded. To her surprise, Principal Beecher was on the line. Without hesitation, he launched into an update on the four teenagers she'd caught skipping school. The conversation ended with him thanking her for suggesting the Garrett go to work for Karl Wilcox. "And, your dad is taking David Cagnalia under his wing," Beecher finished.

Now both retributions were school-sanctioned. Good.

An hour later, Elise knocked on the door for personal visit number one. Instead of a trailer, a government-designed, single-story detached mud brown house housed the Ouray family. Of their five children, only one remained. Elise was here to talk about him.

Neither parent met her eyes as she followed them into a clean but slightly cluttered living room.

"Thank you for making time to see me today," she said.

They merely exchanged looks with each other, on guard, probably wishing she were gone.

Most of her personal visits were to people who wished she'd disappear. Some, of course, were people who hoped she'd help them work the system. What kept her going were the few who welcomed her and asked, "How can this change?"

Change was a good thing.

She sat on a lime-green chair, laid her purse on the old, mud-colored carpeting and opened the folder marked Ouray. As it was a common Ute name, she'd penciled in their initials, too. Then she studied the two people sitting on the couch. Their son, a thirteen-year-old seventh grader, had missed thirteen days of school and it was only November.

"Mr. Ouray, I understand that Clint has stomachaches, but unless you want to be fined or face jail time, he needs to attend class."

Immediately, Elise wanted her words back. Threats only put people on the defensive, and these two might be the highlight of her day. For one, they loved their son. For two, they had agreed to meet her when she called; meaning, they too wanted change even if they didn't know how to make it happen.

An hour later, Elise left the Ouray home feeling she'd accomplished little but empty promises, and headed for personal visit number two.

It was six o'clock by the time she made it to her final stop: Cobre Valley Regional Medical Center. If she'd known what awaited her, she'd have come here first. Tammi Whitefeather was bent on self-destruction. This was her third hospital visit in a year. Each time, the scenario worsened. Her little sister Wynita, watching Elise with red-rimmed eyes, knew it. The nurse still monitoring Tammi's vital signs knew it, and Elise knew it.

Tammi was killing herself with drugs and alcohol, slowly but surely.

Tammi was the age Cindy had been when she died after her drunken boyfriend slammed his car into a tree.

Closing her eyes, Elise thought back ten years to bright hospital lights, gray echoing halls and the smell of hopelessness.

Yes, hopelessness had a smell. Elise hated it. Just like she hated hospitals and the memories they resurrected of showing up, heart in her throat, only to learn that she was too late—Cindy was already dead. Had died less than an hour after sending Elise the text message reading B is drunk. Cm gt me. I dnt want 2 b with him. We @ the rodeo grounds.

If Elise had just read the message sooner, made Cindy a priority, Cindy might still be alive today.

"I think somebody gave her something funny," Wynita said.

The nurse, who knew Elise well from other visits, said, "Heroin."

There'd be forms to fill out, the two-year-old to consider, and judging by Wynita's bulging stomach, soon a third baby to add to the Whitefeathers' folder.

"Your family on the way?" Elise asked.

"I called them, but I don't think they can come. Everyone's busy." Tammi's first hospitalization had brought the whole family, about thirty, to her hospital room. The one after her birthday in June brought about ten. Today, there was just her younger sister.

Elise had gone into social services to make a difference. Clearly, she was failing.

It was almost eight when she got back to the office, and both her coworkers were already gone. Rachel still worked at her desk in the front office.

"Hear anything?" Elise asked. Everyone was concerned about the pending layoff. Who and how many?

"We won't know until next Monday."

Made sense, Elise thought. Holidays were hard times for many struggling people. To most of Elise's clients, and to Elise herself, Thanksgiving wasn't about pilgrims and a shared meal. It was about giving thanks for every day. It was nice that many got a day off to be with family. However, during that family time, much could happen. And, as Elise didn't have family in the area, and chose not to go home this year, she'd be the first one called in the event of an emergency.

The last four years, she'd wanted it that way. This year felt a little off. She didn't know if that was because she'd just visited home and had seen what Cook had planned for Thanksgiving. From what Eva said, they were booked solid on Thanksgiving and a full meal would be offered to all the guests. Both Eva and Emily would be waitressing while Elise stayed in Two Mules alone.

But someone might need her.

Tuesday, Tammi got out of the hospital. Wednesday, a call to the school revealed that Clint Ouray had attended both Tuesday and Wednesday. The Sakiestewas showed up for a counseling late Wednesday afternoon.

"Both claim they're doing fine," Tina said cautiously. "It's a beginning." After four years, her boss was amazed at Elise's continued hopefulness.

It was the only weapon Elise had to battle hopelessness.

"I'm just happy that they actually attended." After making a notation in her computer log, Elise shut down her terminal and followed her boss out the door. Thursday and Friday, no calls came in for assistance so Elise spent the time at the Morningdoves' place, helping with the baby and discussing their planned rodeo club with Randall. She'd drawn him a picture of where the arena should be and what it should look like. She also wrote a projection of what ten longhorn steers would cost and how they'd fund it.

He called her a dreamer.

On Saturday morning, she went to the Two Mules library, housed in a two-room home. The garage acted as an office. The enclosed patio had tables and Elise had started a homework club in the space four months ago. Even though it was a holiday weekend, two students showed up for help. As did three mentors. Elise happily did paperwork while two students got more help than they expected. She also started talking up the rodeo club, taking down names of those interested.

It was the type of morning that kept Elise going.

Tina, at the office, said that creating a program which only helped a few was a waste of time, but Elise thought that success was a road that you paved as you went. Sometimes you could only take one step at a time, but all those steps added up, getting you that much closer to where you wanted to be.

Riding Pistol last week had obviously put her in the mood to ride, so Sunday she headed out to Randall Morningdove's place, borrowed her favorite horse and took off on a long ride.

Monday morning, Elise sat down at her desk and checked her online calendar. Tina came and sat next to her, staring at her feet, then at the floor, before finally looking at Elise and frowning.

"It's official, and I'm the one let go?" Elise whispered.

"You have the least seniority."

"I've got kids who need me." Tammi Whitefeather called almost every day. She was afraid that she'd lose her daughter and the new baby. Tammi's little sister Wynita hadn't called yet to talk to Elise about her own pregnancy, but Elise had called her, three times.

Tina handed her a folder. "I've put a letter of recommendation in there. You visited Apache Creek last week, and they made you a job offer, right?"

Elise stared at her, searching for something to say. But there was no explanation she could give. She'd not shared why she'd left home nor why she'd chosen social work. She'd not told her boss why Apache Creek was no longer home.

"It's not the right fit."

"Sometimes it's the unexpected that brings the most joy." Someone else, Elise couldn't remember who, had said much the same.

"I've got kids who need me. Wynita—"

"We're dividing up your load. You had twenty-one active files."

"What about Randall Morningdove and getting the after-school program using horses—"

"If he wants to run it himself, he's welcome to do so."

"And the tutoring on Saturdays?"

"We'll keep it going as long as the volunteers show up."

"There has to be a go-to person. You'll stay on top of it?"

"I'll do what I can."

Later that night, Elise sat on the front steps of her

mobile home, both dogs at her feet, and stared at the stars. She didn't feel calm; she didn't want to think. What she wanted was a do-over.

Chapter Six

"I don't just plant cotton." Karl Wilcox's gravelly, defensive voice carried across the empty field.

Cooper leaned against his truck, half convinced he needed to leave Garrett alone to atone for his sins and half convinced that Karl was too much for his little brother. Garrett appeared a bit bug-eyed and lost. He kept looking from side to side. No doubt he still thought his friend David would show up to help.

If he did, Cooper would be surprised.

"I've not had any help for a while, but any other year," Karl continued, "I'd have beets, broccoli and spinach going."

Garrett stopped looking around and instead looked at his feet. "Where?"

"Right where you're standing."

"I've driven by here every December for three years, and I've never noticed any vegetables." Garrett, surprisingly, didn't sound rude—just curious.

Cooper kept his mouth closed. He'd driven by for the last fifteen years and hadn't noticed a vegetable crop, either. Just an underutilized farm with two buildings.

"When you're old, you make choices. I've chosen to let the ground rest. We farmers call it rotation."

"Except for cotton?" Garrett asked.

"Except for cotton." Karl nodded. "Right now it's a good cash crop."

That piece of information made Garrett stand a little taller. Cooper knew that Garrett was starting to get uncomfortable asking his mother for extra money, and he wouldn't ask Cooper because Cooper would say, "You get paid by the hour. Use your own money." Plus, after that conversation, Cooper would start querying Garrett about how his paycheck was being spent because it sure wasn't going into savings.

"Sure enough." Karl seemed to stand taller, too. Unfortunately, age worked against him, and he seemed to tilt forward. It didn't stop him, though. This was day six and Cooper's first chance to come see how it was going. Garrett had worked for the man every day after school last week, cleaning out some old barn. This week would be different, working outdoors. Karl was an interesting man, always wearing a yellow flop hat and work clothes: T-shirt and baggy blue jeans. He had a mustache and beard, but Cooper didn't think he had much hair under the hat.

A blue truck came down the road, going fast, and slowed when it came to where the men stood. Instead of traveling past, it pulled off the dirt road and parked in the dirt by Cooper's truck. Elise got out.

Garrett muttered under his breath. Karl shook his head and also muttered, "Getting crowded. Got me a new neighbor down the road. Thinks she can restore the old Simon place alone. Lately, too many females flocking around, and here's one more."

"That's Elise Hubrecht," Garrett said. "She's the one who caught me in your field. It was her idea I work for you."

"I knew her mother." Karl turned back to Garrett. He continued as if Elise hadn't joined them. "Arizona has the best cotton, the whitest, so it's in demand. We don't get enough rain so we rely on irrigation. You'll be repairing part of the drip irrigation system you destroyed. Your brother there will be paying for the parts."

"Hi." Elise walked up and stopped beside Cooper.

He nodded a greeting. He had things to do back at the store and checking up on his little brother took up a lot of his time. He didn't need to add Elise to his list of things to do. No, it was best to keep this professional.

"Just making sure Garrett's doing what he's supposed to be doing," he said.

Not that Garrett wanted his brother to act as a chaperone and supervisor. Unfortunately, want and need were two different things. Truthfully, Cooper didn't mind spending time with his little brother. He just wished he knew what to do to get through to Garrett, help him get past this rough stage. Nothing he did seemed to work.

He hoped working the field with Wilcox would help.

Beside him, Elise shifted from one foot to the other, a half smile on her face. She was pretending to be oblivious to Garrett's and Karl's less than enthusiastic reception. It was a tactic she'd used in the arena when she was trying not to notice and get nervous by how many people were there to watch her ride. She also used to hum "Kum Ba Yah."

He waited to hear if she'd start humming; she didn't.

"Miss Hubrecht," Karl finally acknowledged.

Garrett didn't bother to look at her.

Elise left Cooper's side and carefully walked over the broken dirt. When she made it to Karl, she held out her hand. "Good to see you, Karl. My mom used to drive me by your fields and say that you grew the cotton that I tried to spin on her hand spindle. I wasn't very good."

Karl barely nodded. He didn't reach for her hand to shake.

"My dad always says," she went on, "that you were the best checker player in town. Still play?"

"Not in a long time." With that, Karl went back to giving Garrett instructions, both of them looking as if they'd rather be working than talking with Elise.

"I don't think he likes me," Elise whispered, coming back to lean against the truck and talk to Cooper.

"I don't think he likes anyone."

She nodded but didn't say anything else. Cooper had always been able to tell when something had her feeling pensive, so he gave her an opening. "Back in town so soon? You were just here."

"And I'll be here for a while. I got laid off, so I'm moving back home and taking that job at the high school."

"Sorry to hear that."

"Sorry to hear I got laid off or sorry to hear I'm moving back home?"

"Laid off. I could tell just from what little you told me last week that you loved your job. It's not easy making a change. Up until a year ago, I worked in Moab, Utah. I was just beginning to make friends and a life for myself."

"You came because your family needed you." Elise pointed out. "There's a difference."

"Didn't make it any easier."

"You're right. I guess I'm feeling a little out of place. I just loaded all my personal stuff into Eva's room. One of the cabins empties next week, and I'll be staying there for a while. I knew it was coming."

"You said you'd be looking for work near Two Mules."

"There is no work. I knew what was coming and spent the last month checking out the job market and letting the world know my availability."

"So Apache Creek High School is your only option, whether you like it or not?"

The wind picked up, blowing her hair across her face. She pushed it back before she answered. "It's the option I'm accepting. I'm on my way over to officially tell the principal I'll be taking the job. I just saw you guys here and wanted to see how it was going."

"It's going fine. He's taking it better than I thought he would." Cooper tried not to let it bother him that Apache Creek was a last resort. The Elise he knew had loved it here.

Looking at Elise, her hair fanning in the wind and her dark eyes so solemn, he had to push aside the frustration that threatened to bubble. When Cindy's boyfriend, Brandon, got behind the wheel of his car after drinking, he'd probably not thought of the collateral damage he was about to inflict on his family and friends. Brandon had survived the crash, but like Elise, he had left town shortly after. Unlike Elise, he went far away and never came back.

It was wrong, just plain wrong, that Elise didn't feel excited about moving back home. Just as much as it had been wrong, just plain wrong, for her to walk away from him, from the life they'd planned. He hated that Cindy died, too. They'd been friends for years. He'd helped teach Cindy to drive. He blamed himself, too, for—

"But really." Elise interrupted his thoughts, bringing him back down to earth and to the issue at hand. "This job is tailor-made for me. It's what I've really wanted to do all along. To work in a school, I mean. I had some really great ideas in Two Mules about tutoring and starting a riding club, but nobody got excited about them but me and a few students. If I could have had backing, I think the kids would have benefited in the long run."

He put his hands in his pockets and leaned back against his truck. Karl was showing his brother how to use a hoe. It was slow-going and all Cooper could do not to hurry out and help.

She continued, talking more to herself than him. "I did manage to start a tutoring program. The school already had one in place, but I wanted one that was a little more individualized—one-on-one instead of in a group. I managed to get the Two Mules Public Library to host it on Saturday mornings."

"Two Mules is big enough for a library?"

"Every town should have a library. And one that hosts after-school tutoring every day."

Tutoring was something that Cooper had never really had reason to think about. School had come easy to him, until he'd been distracted by Elise. "So, you going to stay here until summer, then look for something else?" He'd not known he was going to ask the question until it popped out.

"They'll probably expect me to sign a one-year contract."

And then she'd go. He could survive with her in the

area for a year. He just needed to make sure to not be where she was. Those raw feelings he was pushing aside weren't getting the hint. "Your dad must be happy."

She laughed and leaned back against the truck beside him. He could see the worry around her eyes, but he could also see determination.

"That he is. Before we settled on letting me live in one of the cabins, he offered to move out of the apartment over the barn and let me have it. That would put him back in the main house. I thought Eva would faint at the idea."

"I don't imagine it would be easy as a new bride to have your father living with you."

"Some fathers, maybe it wouldn't be a problem," Elise allowed. "Our father, not a chance. Eva's house will be finished in a few months. It will be easier then."

"Do you remember the time he caught us kissing in Pistol's stall?"

"I remember that he took my cell phone for two weeks."

"I don't know why he was so mad. It's not like we were doing anything but kissing."

But Cooper knew what had scared Jacob Hubrecht. It had been the sight of his daughter with Cooper, so very comfortable, and clearly in love, so very young and growing up.

The man just hadn't known that he had nothing to worry about—not for long, anyway. It was only a few months after that that Cindy had died, and Elise had left Cooper behind for good. The woman she was now, the one that she had grown into in the years since then… wasn't Cooper's anymore. And he was sure she never would be again.

* * *

Just before heading back to her truck, she and Cooper had exchanged phone numbers for Garrett's sake. It felt funny adding his name to her contacts. She took down Garrett's number, too.

Working for Karl wouldn't be easy for the sullen teen. But after watching the two—Garrett and Karl— she was convinced they might be good for each other. Garrett could use an adult male role model who wasn't a relative and Karl needed help on his place. It had been painful to watch him hold the hoe.

As she drove to the high school, she reminded herself that she'd always wanted to work with teens in a place where there was a sense of community. It would be hard enough coming back to Apache Creek and seeing her old haunts and facing Cindy's absence.

Just as difficult was facing Cooper's presence. Away from Apache Creek, it had been easy to push memories of Cindy and Cooper away. But while she was here, they both kept filling her thoughts. The memories of what he used to mean to her—what they used to mean to each other—made her ache for what they had lost. But at the same time, she still felt the urge to pull away from him, just as she had after Cindy died. Deep down, she'd felt—then and now—that she didn't have the right to be as happy as Cooper used to make her when Cindy wasn't alive to find happiness, too. It was a feeling that almost brought her to her knees.

Which might be where she belonged.

She hadn't prayed, really prayed, in years. Oh, she prayed for other people. She prayed for and with her clients, but she'd not said a prayer for herself in more than ten years. In the back of her mind she wondered if she had prayed, then maybe she could have forgiven herself and gone on with Cooper to live the life they'd wanted.

Now it was big city or small town and swallow pride.

"I'll take the job." Elise stood in Principal Beecher's office.

It took two days for Apache Creek High School to approve and file the proper paperwork. On Wednesday, Elise had her own office, very different from her tiny cubicle in Two Mules. Her first email awaited, sent a day before she was hired, and contained the names of seventy-two students. These were the ones that Principal Beecher considered a top priority.

"When you've settled those, I'll give you the second wave," he promised.

There were more than seventy-two problem cases in the school? And, she wasn't quite sure what he meant by *settled*. Or, how much time he was giving her. In just a few weeks, it would be Christmas vacation. She also wasn't sure why Jasmine Taylor's name, as well as photo, was the top one. Finding a runaway was a bit more than Elise could do. It took her an hour to set up her computer the way she wanted it. After that, she read through the seventy-plus files, organizing them by her first impression of their degrees of need. After that, she compared need to current GPA grades, contrasting back at least two semesters. Then she considered family situation and address.

Two students didn't even have an address.

More than a few could benefit from a tutoring opportunity like the one she'd started in Two Mules. Elise made a mental note to stop by the local library. Sometimes it just took being off the school's campus to create a feeling of a safe environment. She was surprised how few of the students were involved in clubs. She'd have to figure out what was being offered and see if she could match students to opportunities.

As she ate her lunch, she noted the last names on her list. She knew more than three fourths of the families. She finished the ham-and-cheese sandwich—drizzled with ketchup just the way she liked—and started in on the bag of potato chips. Because she had her figure to consider, she also ate the four baby carrots. Yuck. Great, just great, file number seventy-two was Sophia Hamm. Cindy's younger sister, just five years old when Cindy died. She'd been the baby, then. But there was another daughter now, currently age eight. Elise's father had once commented that he thought the Hamms had the little girl to help stave off the pain of Cindy's loss.

Elise didn't disagree.

She made a notation on Sophia's document and thought to herself that the Hamms having another child made a whole lot more sense than Tammi Whitefeather having a baby at fifteen and another at seventeen. But she wasn't here to judge, just to assist.

Feeling a little humbled at how intimate it felt to be working with families she'd known all her life, Elise sat back and took the final morsel from her lunch. Cook only packed two chocolate chip cookies. Well, the guests only got one cookie. Cook put in the second just for her, a sort of "Welcome Home" offering. The way things were going, Elise could really use a few more.

She looked at the names on the files again. Principal Beecher had done a good job. Elise definitely wanted to find out what was going on with all of them, but there were five she wanted to target first. And, she wasn't following them in his order. She headed for Miss Sadie. It was an hour after lunch, and Elise doubted the school counselor would be busy so close to dismissal.

"Come in, come in." Sadie stood up. When Elise was in school, everyone talked about how Miss Sadie always wore clothes that matched. Today was no different. She wore a blue-and-white checked blouse. The blue matched both her pants and sweater. Her white tennis shoes had laces the same shade of blue as her shirt. Even the tips of her reading glasses were blue.

"I'm glad you're still here," Elise said. "You were always my favorite person to talk to."

"You," Sadie accused, "didn't talk enough. Yup, you always knew exactly what you wanted."

She didn't add "up until the end."

"Maybe my problem was that I was so focused, I didn't know how to react when my plans got derailed."

"Spoken like a true psychologist." Sadie leaned back in her chair and nodded, seemingly pleased with the way the conversation went.

"I've a four-year degree in social work with an emphasis on child development. I didn't go the psychology path."

"It found you anyway."

Elise opened her iPad and found her page. "I wonder if you have time for a few questions."

"If it's about our students, I have all the time you need."

Elise glanced down at the five names she'd typed. Sadie knew them all. The two without addresses were homeless. One was staying with relatives, and the other was living with his family in their car.

"But—"

"If you call Mathias in and bring up the situation,

he'll shut down. He's embarrassed. Right now school is all he has that feels normal. I've tried to gently suggest avenues that will help, but when I do, he tends to miss the next day and avoid me for a week or more. If I let him come to me, which is rare, I can get him to take food home with him, and I can answer a few homework questions. He had a group project a few months ago that gave him grief. Looking back, I wish I'd spoken to the teacher about pairing Mathias with David Cagnalia. David's a good boy but high-spirited. Jasmine Taylor was the other team member, and she certainly wasn't the type to maintain order. Right now basketball is the only thing he's excited about."

Maybe Apache Creek didn't need a social worker. Maybe Sadie was enough.

"What else do you know about Jasmine Taylor?"

"I'm completely flummoxed. The girl had straight A's and a bright future ahead of her. Her parents call me every other day just in case I've heard something. If you'd asked me to line kids up in the hallway from most likely to run away to least likely, she'd have been at the end of the line.

The next two kids Elise asked about were special needs.

"But never tested," Sadie said. "The parents refuse to consider that something is wrong. Without an IEP, we can't help them the way they truly need."

Back in Two Mules, Gina Morningdove had been on an IEP, an Individualized Education Program. She'd been provided with extra tutoring and more time to complete tests.

These were the five Elise knew she needed to deal

with first. She started to turn off the iPad but hesitated. "What about Garrett Smith?"

Miss Sadie didn't blink at the question. "Last year, Garrett started hanging around David Cagnalia. At first, I didn't notice a change, but after a few months Garrett's grades dropped, his attitude got surly, and he's missed a lot more school. More than his brother knows."

"Don't you mean mother?"

"Karen's not been feeling well. Lately, when the school calls, she's in bed. Garrett's taken advantage of this. Cooper's doing more and more." Sadie leaned forward. "Quite honestly, he's doing the best he knows how, but everything's landed on his shoulders. He could really use help."

Cooper was trying; Elise knew that for a fact. There'd not been many cases where Elise made a recommendation for contribution and a family member showed up to watch. Cooper had. He'd been standing by the truck, making sure his little brother did what he was supposed to do.

Unaware of Elise's thoughts, Sadie continued. "We call home when Garrett doesn't show up. The teachers have conferences over grades. And, now we've hired you. Garrett is a smart boy. He knows how to avoid getting caught. I think you're probably the best thing to happen to him in a year and half. I hear he's had to clean up the mess he made at Karl's."

"Yes, I've seen him there. You know Karl?"

"Went to school with him. He was best friends with my brother."

"He was always a grouch when my sisters and I strayed too close to his land."

"You know," Sadie said, "the fact that he agreed to

let Garrett repair the damage is just as much a healing for him as it is an opportunity for Garrett."

"How do you mean?"

"For Garrett, he'll be working alongside an adult male who is not his brother."

"There's probably some resentment there," Elise agreed. "With their father gone, Cooper's trying to fill a role Garrett never wanted emptied."

"You said it better than I could. That's why we need you here."

They spent some more time on Elise's files. Finally, Sadie looked at the clock, inspiring Elise to do the same.

Amazing, it was after three. Elise hadn't heard the dismissal bell nor the noise of three hundred students trying to hustle out the door.

"I've a three-thirty appointment with a home-schooled student wanting some advice on college," Sadie said. "We can continue this conversation tomorrow."

Elise almost picked up her iPad and left, but there was one more thing. "You said having Garrett there to help out would be healing for Karl. What did you mean?"

"Karl had a son who ran away during his senior year." Elise's jaw dropped open, but Sadie wasn't done. "Before that, Karl was a contributing member of society. He attended church, supplied food to some of the shelters, and even volunteered at the arthritis center. After Billy ran away, he got divorced and became a hermit. Sad, sad thing." Sadie looked up. "It's why Principal Beecher put Jasmine Taylor's name first on your list."

"But—"

Someone knocked at the door. It opened an inch and a young blonde with a notebook and pencil peeked in. "Miss Sadie, is it time for my appointment?"

A moment later, Elise headed back to her office wondering how exactly Miss Sadie knew that Principal Beecher had put Jasmine first on the list.

The problem with small towns, Cooper thought, was assumptions. Elise had only been in her position just over a week, and already people assumed that he either knew her every move or wanted to know about her every move.

"You hear Elise took on Coach Butler?" This piece of news came on Friday at three o'clock by way of Sam Miller, a police officer a little older than Cooper.

"You're kidding." Now this might be newsworthy. Cooper repositioned a Christmas list in Santa's hand. The Santa figure was bent near a trough and also holding a panning bowl. It was the second week of December, and Cooper was still repositioning his holiday decorations. His mother, for some strange reason, had put the Santa near the door, propped against the wall, not even standing. It looked like Santa had entered AJ's Outfitters and promptly collapsed against the wall to rest. Not exactly the impression Cooper wanted Santa to give about panning for gold!

"I guess after school yesterday, she attended basketball practice."

"Elise likes sports. She came to all my practices."

"She liked *you*. She didn't care what sport." Sam bent down and looked at Santa's face. "His nose is a little funny-looking."

"Mom dropped him twice while she dragged him in here."

"Why didn't you carry him in here yourself?"

"I didn't know she was doing it because I was picking Garrett up from school. I thought I had enough Christmas cheer in the store." To make his point, Cooper stared pointedly at the tool-laden wreaths, the Christmas tree in the corner and the Santa figures placed strategically throughout the store. There was even a sprig of mistletoe hanging from the door frame between the office and counter. "I guess not. It's the price I pay for taking away Garrett's keys to the truck."

"You're late then."

"What?"

"It's after three. If he doesn't have his truck anymore then shouldn't you be picking him up?"

"He's been working at Karl Wilcox's after class. He's still paying off his debt to the man." Cooper tried to readjust Santa's nose, but it wasn't really bent. Instead, when his mom dropped Santa, some of the paint had peeled off the nose leaving the white, hard plastic exposed. Anywhere else and Cooper might have tried to cover it with some fake snow. As it was, he adjusted Santa's beard.

"So," Cooper said, when Santa was finally looking as if he was ready to strike it rich: rock hammer in hand and surrounded by the accessories every competent gold-panning Santa would need. "Why is Elise taking on Coach Butler?"

"Apparently she isn't impressed with his techniques."

Probably from being a cop, Sam had the habit of dropping a tidbit and then waiting for either a reaction or new information. For the last week, Cooper had been merely nodding and smiling when his customers brought up Elise. Most took the hint and allowed him to change the subject. Others liked to tease; Cooper didn't smile. Still, he knew how to play Sam's game. "And what wasn't she impressed with and why did she attend?"

"She attended because of a student. At least that's my guess. I can think of one or two who might need the guidance of a social worker. And, she wasn't impressed with the way the coach yelled at the players. That's a fact, not a guess. Coach Butler is very vocal. It takes some getting used to."

"How do you know all this?"

"I stopped by the school yesterday to talk to one of the students about the Jasmine Taylor case. I overheard some of the kids talking. I guess Elise actually got on the court."

Cooper would have liked to have seen that.

Sam continued. "One of the players missed an easy shot and the coach really reamed him."

"Hmm. Elise knows that coaches ream students all the time. Her dad was a master at it."

"I was thinking the same thing. Still, I wish I'd been a fly on the wall to see her go after the coach."

"You probably wish that a lot. You'd solve a lot more cases and quicker."

Sam laughed, but soon sobered. "I can't make up my mind if this coach is out of line or just old-school. Got me thinking. You've got the five boys from church who always go panning with you. Any of them play basketball? I'd like to get an opinion."

"I don't think any of them are on the team," Cooper said. "They'd have invited me to a game. Come to think of it, for the last few years John Stanford's been a player. But he's not invited me to a game recently. I wonder…" Cooper took his phone from his belt.

"Could be John got busy and decided to drop sports and focus on his schoolwork," Sam mused. "He's a serious kid."

Cooper didn't think that was it. John was the kind of kid who knew how to manage his time, and if he wanted to play basketball, he'd have made time. Then, too, "Garrett talked about trying out two years ago. I don't remember if he did or not. I was working in Moab." Cooper texted John while listening to Sam. You play basketball this year?

"That would have been Abe Butler's first year," Sam remembered. "What was Garrett thinking choosing basketball over football?"

"He didn't—he kept up with football his freshman year, but when Coach Nelson retired before Garrett's sophomore year, football got dropped, too. I'm not sure I know Coach Butler. He doesn't attend our church, and he's not done any business here."

No, came a quick return text.

"Not surprising," Sam said. "He's an old man, a bit rigid. I've been out to his house once or twice when he's called in a complaint. He lives next door to the Cagnalias."

"Now that's worth knowing." Cooper finished texting a Why? and greeted a couple who came in the door. "Can I help you?"

"We're new to the area and keep driving by," the man said. "We thought we'd check it out." They looked a bit lost and headed over to the corner where he had books.

"Look for *Gold Mining of the Twenty-First Century*," Cooper advised. "It's the go-to book in the Southwest."

"Thanks."

"We have a group of people who go out panning after rain, too," Cooper added. "If you're interested in coming along, let me know and I'll put your name on the contact list. Take your time looking around. If you have any questions, let me know."

Sam came and leaned on the counter, lowered his voice, and continued, "Nelson would be a hard act to follow."

Cooper tried to think about the past year. Garrett certainly wasn't talking up the games. Neither were his regular customers.

"What's the past season been like?"

"Pretty good. But then the Apache Creek Bears have always been good."

No time, John texted back.

Cooper handed Sam his phone and watched as the officer read the words. Before he could ask for an opinion, Cooper's cell phone rang. Sam handed it over, and Cooper checked the number and took the call.

"Is Garrett there?" David Cagnalia sounded upset.

"No." Not a chance Cooper would tell David to go over to the Wilcox place to find his brother. David would just be a distraction for Garrett and might annoy Karl.

"He was supposed to meet me ten minutes ago."

"Really?" Now Cooper was concerned. "Are you sure? Because he had plans after school."

"Ah, never mind. I shouldn't have called." David hung up before Cooper could say anything else. Looking at his phone, Cooper shook his head. He had a bad feeling about this.

Almost immediately, his phone rang again. This time he didn't recognize the number except that it was local.

"Cooper Smith," he answered, expecting a sales call.

He didn't get one.

"Cooper, this is Elise. Your brother's in trouble. You might want to get over here."

Chapter Seven

When Elise got the phone call from Karl, she almost fell off her chair. After instructing Karl to call the police, she dialed Cooper and then cleared her appointed schedule—not an easy task—before shooting out the door. She'd also mentally reprioritized her students. Now Garrett took the first-place position on her list.

As she drove to the farm, she scolded herself, thinking that if Garrett had been a top priority from the start, as she'd suspected he might need to be, maybe he'd not be in trouble today.

Foolish thinking. He'd been getting in trouble all year. The police chief beat her to the Wilcox place and was questioning Karl when she arrived. Karl was going on and on about what could have motivated Garrett to take thirty dollars and a box of food. The police chief was intent on finding Garrett before he got into even more trouble. Elise stepped closer, ready to fill in important information. She'd seen Garrett this morning, knew what he was wearing, knew who his friends were. A moment later, however, a patrol officer returned with a highly agitated Garrett in tow. Maybe it was the insolent look on Garrett's face or the way he slouched, but suddenly all Karl would say was "Get him off my property."

Then, when Karl started to get upset, Chief Fisher moved them to the police station.

"Do you need me to tag along?" Elise asked.

He gave a curt nod. Thirty minutes later, Elise sat in a chair next to Garrett and wished Cooper would hurry up and get here. She couldn't help but like the chief of police. He had not only his own certificates and awards scattered throughout his office but also movie posters. His favorite movie seemed to be *X-Men* and all things Wolverine. A shelf by the back of the room had at least a dozen action figures.

She'd never been in the Apache Creek police station before. It was small, the same size as the one in Two Mules. Now that one she'd been in, at least once a week in the four years she'd worked there. Both stations had the same decorator: wanted pictures on the bulletin board, ugly green chairs in the waiting room and outdated magazines. Walking down the hallway from the waiting room to the chief's office was a Hall of Fame. The walls, painted a sick gray color, were decorated with portraits of past sheriffs and the current one. At the end, one whole wall was a memorial to the only law officer in Apache Creek to be killed in the line of duty.

Elise didn't remember him.

Unlike Two Mules, though, the Apache Creek police station was clean, almost sterile.

Didn't matter. She hated the fact that she was here at all, hated that Garrett was rebelling in such a destructive way. She was a bit mad at herself. She'd been so busy with other duties that she hadn't given Garrett any time yet. He was on her list of things to do.

A long list.

On the other hand, his brother was on her list of things to avoid: avoid looking for his truck driving down the street, avoid looking for him coming out of the convenience store on her way to work, avoid looking for him in the school hallway in case he was there for Garrett.

She'd neglected to add avoid seeing him at the police station, but finally he joined their little party.

"Sorry it took me so long to get here. I went to Karl Wilcox's place first." Sitting across from his brother, Cooper looked like a wounded animal ready to spring. He was that mad. "Tell me you didn't steal from Karl Wilcox," he demanded.

His mother was in a chair right next to Garrett. She kept rubbing her hands, a nervous reaction that Elise hadn't seen before.

"Tell them exactly what you told me." Chief Fisher looked at Elise.

"Mr. Wilcox called me at about 3:35. He said that Garrett had shown up right after school, started in without needing guidance, and that twenty minutes later, Garrett went into the house to get something cold to drink. He came back, went to work. When Mr. Wilcox stopped working to rest, a few minutes later, Garrett did, too. Next thing Karl knew, Garrett had left without saying why. Karl was annoyed—"

"—rightly so," interjected Cooper, giving Garrett a seething look.

Elise continued "—and went in the house to get your

phone number. That's when he noticed that the drawer of his nightstand was open."

"Which is where Karl kept some money," Chief Fisher stated. "About thirty dollars. Well, he had ten just laying on top, where it could be plainly seen. Twenty more inside."

"Why did Karl call you instead of us?" Cooper asked Elise.

"I think I'm the first number he found. I'm now the person listed as the liaison between the school and the hours of community service Garrett is performing."

"I didn't know this was community service," Cooper protested. "I thought we were just following a suggestion made by a fri—" His sentence trailed off and Elise had to force herself not to wince.

He'd almost said friend.

Well, maybe she was still a friend, but it was debatable, and based on the expression on his face, she'd not earned any points in her favor today.

"Once I took the position at Apache Creek High," she explained, "I became responsible for overseeing the students on my caseload."

"And Garrett's a part of your caseload?" Cooper didn't look happy.

Chief Fisher joined in. "Because Garrett is working at the Wilcox place as a consequence of activities done during school hours, yes, he's part of her caseload. But we're getting sidetracked here. Garrett, what did you plan to do with the food and money?"

"It was only thirty bucks. I've worked hard enough for it."

"You took it from the man's dresser drawer," Chief Fisher stated. "Not only that, it wasn't in plain sight, so you were hunting for it. Then there's the food you pilfered, too."

"You arresting me?" Garrett asked.

"Should I?" Fisher responded.

"No," Cooper exploded. "We'll repay the money, with interest, if need be. And we'll deal with this."

His mother leaned forward, no longer rubbing her fingers. "Cooper, I want you to head back to the store. Friday afternoons are busy. You're needed there. I can take care of this."

"Mom, you need—"

Elise really looked at Karen Smith. The woman had been like a mother to her at one time, one sorely needed by the tomboy daughter of an ex-rodeoer who thought morning and night ended on the back of a horse.

"Garrett and I will deal with this. Thank you." Now Karen's hands clutched her purse, which sat in her lap. Her hands were slightly red, slightly swollen and slightly twisted.

Elise studied Cooper. He never once looked anywhere but at his mother's face and he definitely wasn't happy about being dismissed, but he stood and then, after giving his brother a look that clearly read "We'll deal with this later," he left.

"Why did you take the food and money?" Karen asked.

Elise took a small step toward the door, wondering if she should leave. As a social worker, she had every right to be here. But, so far, she hadn't been needed. Yet maybe she was needed other ways. She couldn't stop looking at the woman's hands.

"I was planning to meet David and, well, it just happened." Garrett was lying. Elise could see it in his eyes.

A quick look at his mother made Elise think that she knew it, too.

"We can't suspend you from school as this was an off-campus infraction." Elise pushed away from the wall and took Cooper's seat. "But, if Karl Wilcox decides to press charges, this will go on your record. Do you understand that, Garrett?"

He looked up from studying the floor. Elise was taken aback. He had his brother's eyes. His hair was the same color, although cut a lot shorter than Cooper ever kept his. And his eyes were full of pain. The same kind of pain she'd put in his big brother's.

"I understand." Garrett's words were curt, his tone surly.

"I'll talk with Karl," his mother said. "We'll take care of this. You can count on it." Karen looked across at her son. "I'll be driving the truck home. You've lost all driving privileges. Cooper and I will be taking you wherever you need to be—home, school and possibly Karl's place. If he'll take you back."

"Mom, I—"

"I take it—" Karen paid no attention to Garrett's pleading tone, and looked at Chief Fisher "—that Karl didn't accompany you to the station?"

"I told him I'd be by later to take a report."

"You have any objection to my talking to him first?"

Chief Fisher shook his head. "I didn't get the impression he intended to press charges. But I got the idea that Garrett is no longer welcome there."

"Head out to the truck," Karen told her son. Garrett quickly left the room.

"Elise, thank you for coming. I might stop by the school early next week. I'd like to hear about this community service you've assigned him. Maybe there's something else he can do."

"You want me to change him from Karl's place to somewhere else?"

"No, I intend to talk Karl into keeping him busier than he's ever dreamed."

Elise walked over to Karen and bent down to take her by the elbow and help her up. Luckily, Karen moved fairly quickly and was out the office door in two steps. Elise stayed right by her. When they got to the hallway and the door shut behind them, Elise said, "I don't have a medical degree and cannot diagnose, but if I did, I'd say to you, 'So, does Cooper know you have arthritis and how bad it is?'"

Karen pursed her lips and then let out a breath of air. "I'm fine. It's just all the changes since Mitch died."

Elise wanted to say more, but she'd been gone a long time and the rapport she'd had with Karen from years ago was mostly gone. Plus, as her past instructors and even her supervisor back at Two Mules often reminded her, she wasn't a doctor.

"Karen, if you need help—"

"I don't need help. I just need to convince Cooper to stop shouldering all the responsibilities. It's all I can do to convince him *I'm* Garrett's parent. Since Mitch died, well, it's like Cooper's driven. He didn't even tell me you were back. I had to find out during that Saturday ride."

"I wasn't exactly back."

"You'd been in the store the day before. Used to be Cooper told me everything, at least everything that mattered."

Elise closed her eyes, but only for a moment. She

didn't want Karen to think anything was amiss. Or that it bothered her that maybe she didn't matter enough to Cooper anymore to be considered worthy of a mention to his mother.

It was better if she didn't. Then when she left again…

"What's wrong with Garrett?" Karen demanded. "We didn't go through all this with Cooper. Have times really changed? Is he following his peers, being influenced by David Cagnalia? Or, is all this acting out because he lost his father?"

"I wish I could give you a definite answer. Peer pressure is real at any age, and loss is as much a way of life as life itself. Kids do stupid things. Garrett, however, has something too many kids do not have—a support system. He has you. He has Cooper. In Two Mules, I can't tell you how many times I sat with a teenager at the police station and I was his only advocate."

Karen sighed, looking sad but at least a little comforted by Elise's words. "Thank you. It's something to think about. Peer pressure, huh? I suppose there's nothing for us to do but get through it. Thanks again for your help. We appreciate it. I've never been so worried in my life." With that, Karen walked down the hall. Elise by her side, not mentioning again that Karen probably needed to spend some time worrying about herself.

His mother and brother didn't get home until after eight. Cooper was still in a bad mood and trying to shake it off. When they stepped in, though, he saw that his mood was nothing compared to theirs. His brother stomped off to his room, slammed the door, turned the radio on loud, and Cooper knew he'd be there the rest of the night.

His mother, lips pursed, tiredly asked, "Are you hungry?"

"No." Cooper wasn't about to say yes. Somehow he knew that even the act of cooking a light meal would be too much for her right now. She slowly walked through the living room, barely noting his presence on the couch, and to the kitchen table where she laid her purse. Then she lowered herself into the chair. Cooper waited.

When she didn't do anything else, he stood, walked to the kitchen, and, now that he'd had time to think, took out some cans of noodle soup. He might not be hungry, but one thing for sure, his mother needed to eat. She had lost weight in the last year and always seemed to need rest. He poured the soup into a pan and turned on the burner to the stove. Then he went to the table, sat down next to her and, as he'd seen his father do so many times, he put his hands on top of hers.

"Garrett is a great kid. Whatever he's going through now, he'll get over it. You shouldn't compare him to me. I didn't have to deal with losing a parent while still in high school."

"He stole from Karl. There's no excuse."

"So is he done working for Karl? Or were you able to convince him to give Garrett a second chance?"

"He'll keep working for Karl. More than just cleaning up the field. Karl said he had some fence to repair and ditches to dig."

"I'm surprised Karl agreed to it."

"Me, too," his mother admitted. "But really, it makes some sense. Truth is, he agreed not because I asked him. He agreed because he likes Garrett."

"You're kidding." Cooper was amazed.

"No, and it didn't occur to me until I was standing in his living room tonight. That man needs Garrett as much as Garrett needs him."

Cooper didn't think Karl Wilcox needed anyone. He was a loner, and the times Cooper had stopped by to check on Garrett, Karl hadn't said more than ten words to him.

"Karl lost a son many, many years ago." His mother's words were soft, almost whispered, as if this was a memory best forgotten.

"In a war?"

"No, not in that way. I'd forgotten until I stood in Karl's living room and looked at the photos on the wall. Then I remembered my mother talking about why Karl was so unfriendly to us kids. She said he couldn't bear having young people around because it reminded him of what he'd lost."

"That doesn't make any sense."

"Not to you. You've never turned your back on the Lord. Karl did. He forgot that the Lord doesn't make loss easier, but He makes it bearable."

Nothing had been easy since Cooper's dad had gotten sick. Everyone in the Smith family suffered. Cooper wanted to feel empathy for Garrett, but he didn't have time.

"What else do you remember?"

"Mom told me that Karl's son left for school one morning and never came home. I don't remember the whole story—I was only about twelve years old when it happened. I *do* know that when Karl finally headed for the school at six o'clock to try to find out why his son wasn't home yet, no one was there. He went to the principal's house. They started calling teachers and found out that he'd been absent from every class. Back then they didn't report absences quite like they do now, so no one had been notified. Once word spread, the whole town went out looking. Mom said people searched for Karl's son for two months straight."

"How old was he? What was his name?"

"I don't remember exactly, though he had to be eighteen or so. He was a senior. Everyone in town was worried about their kids for years after that. My mother wouldn't let me stay out past ten o'clock on a date until I was almost eighteen—and I always had to check in and let them know where I was. That's how scared parents were. It wasn't until I saw the pictures in Karl's living room that I remembered."

Cooper thought about watching Karl and Garrett in the field. Karl hadn't smiled or laughed even once. Neither had Garrett. There had to be a way to get through to both of them. Garrett, at least, was still going to church. Mostly because his mom made him.

Unbidden came the thought of Elise. She'd been back more than two weeks. Not once had she attended church.

His mother continued, "Used to be, the *Apache Creek Tribune* would run a story every few years about his disappearance. They'd even put in his photo with a what-he-might-look-like-now enhancement. That hasn't happened since Garrett was born."

"I'm surprised they didn't revisit the disappearance after Jasmine went missing," Cooper said.

"Me, too, now that I think of it. Surely that would garner some interest."

With that, she pushed herself up from the table and slowly stood. Her eyes swept the kitchen, then the living room, stopping for a moment on the La-Z-Boy that had been his dad's favorite chair. Finally, she looked down the hall. Together they listened to the music coming from Garrett's room. It was louder than his dad would have allowed, but only by a little. His mother shook her head.

"I'm going to bed. Tomorrow, there will be more to deal with."

Cooper didn't want to go to bed; he wasn't tired. He didn't want to go to his room, either. He didn't feel at home there. It was almost as if he'd been thrust back in time and was grappling for his role in life. He'd been a single professional while living in Moab. Now, his role was son, brother, and, yes, ex-fiancé. It made for a sense of lost control.

Retrieving his laptop, he settled at the kitchen table and logged in, pulling up a search engine. No surprise, Karl Wilcox was a common name. He narrowed it to Apache Creek and found ten matches.

Karl's son was Billy Wilcox. His mother was close to getting the age right. The boy had been seventeen when he'd disappeared. There was a photo depicting a slender brown-haired youth with unruly hair and slightly protruding ears wearing a black T-shirt and jeans. He'd disappeared in 1978. Nearly a decade before Cooper's birth. Almost two decades before Garrett's.

Cooper couldn't really see the resemblance between father and son since the blurry photo his computer showed came from the copied newspaper. Still, he could see what Karl had looked like more than forty years ago, since the newspaper ran photos of him, as well. The woman next to him was identified as Juanita Wilcox. Cooper did a quick search and found out that the couple had divorced in 1979, and then that she'd passed away five years after Billy disappeared.

Never knowing what had happened to her son.

Cooper closed his eyes. No matter what problems Garrett was causing at the moment, at least Cooper knew the kid was in his room, listening to strange music, and probably mad at the world.

There were a dozen stories about Billy's disappearance. He was best known as the boy who ran the produce stand on the side of the road. Cooper thought of how many times he'd been called the boy who dug for gold. Funny, that moniker stopped bothering him once Elise entered his life. Most articles reported that Billy had been a loner. A few, however, mentioned friends. Twenty minutes into reading, he realized the friend mentioned most often was a girl named Naomi Humestewa. The name was familiar.

Elise's mother.

Her family, most of whom did not live in Apache Creek, came down to help with the search. They'd found the only clue to Billy's whereabouts. Way up near the Weaver's Needle in the Superstition Mountains, they'd found Billy's black T-shirt. It was the same color as the rest of the article so Cooper couldn't really make out any markings. According to the reporter, it advertised Grand Funk Railroad. Cooper had no idea who they were. A quick search gave him a rock-and-roll band.

Naomi Humestewa, huh?

There was a quote from Raymond Humestewa, Naomi's brother, Cooper remembered, referring to the mountain as Ka-Katak-Tami. The paper translated it to mean the Crooked Top Mountain. Raymond said that if Billy had gotten lost on the mountain, they needed to be looking for bones instead of a body.

It had been early May when Billy went missing. Hot enough to die from lack of water, but Billy was a hometown boy. If he'd run away, he'd have known what to pack. Unless he'd run away on a whim without any planning in advance. Hard to imagine crusty old Karl raising a boy who'd react on a whim. Cooper read a bit more, trying to find Karl's response to Raymond's prediction.

He found no other information about Billy. What he did find was a desire to befriend Karl.

With a sigh, Cooper left the laptop and headed down the hall to his mother's room. Her door was closed, and the light off. He looked at the clock. It was after ten. Instead of calling Elise, he took out his phone and texted: U awake?

A moment later came: Yes.

Ever heard of Billy Wilcox?

No. Who is he?

Cooper debated. They could do this over text messaging and keep it impersonal. Or, he could call her, but he figured she'd find a way to make the conversation brief.

What are you doing?

Cleaning up after the supper crowd.

The Lost Dutchman Ranch wasn't just a place where a family lived. It was a dude ranch, usually full, especially at Christmas.

Christmas?

Looking around the house, he realized they'd not put up even one decoration—unless he counted the five Christmas cards that had arrived in the mail and that his mother displayed on top of the fireplace mantel. One had fallen on its side.

Feel like some company? he typed.

She didn't respond right away. He waited, thinking about all the years he'd not even asked if she wanted company; instead, he'd just gone over.

Is this about Garrett?

Well, Garrett was working for Karl, so Yes.

Where?

I can come there.

OK.

He stuck his phone back in the case that attached to his belt and went down the hall and into his bedroom for his jacket. The days were perfect this time of year, but the evenings had a bite.

The music sounding from his brother's room hadn't decreased in volume. Cooper couldn't make out the words and wondered why Garrett didn't use his earbuds. Maybe he just wanted to annoy everyone. Cooper lightly tapped on the door. Just in case Garrett came looking for him, he'd say goodbye.

After a moment, he knocked louder. Then he tried the door. It opened and Cooper looked into a room full of skateboard parts, empty food plates, DVD cases and clothes. The computer was on and the music came from it.

Clothes were on the bed, piled in one corner and the middle.

Garrett, however, was gone.

Chapter Eight

Elise arrived at Cooper's house right after Officer Sam Miller. He remained in the patrol car, his mobile data terminal screen glowing in the darkness. She wondered if this was how it had been when Jasmine Taylor had gone missing: calls in the night, patrol cars in the street, every light in the house on and friends rushing over.

Elise knocked gently on the front door and when no one answered, she pushed it open and went in. Just being here, in Cooper's house, made her pause. Nostalgia washed over her, and she froze. It hadn't changed since she'd last been here. It was a male domain. That made sense as Cooper's dad had been an outdoorsman and Cooper and Garrett with him. Karen had gone with the flow, always ready to have fun—camping, rodeo, quad rides, gold panning—as long as it made her men happy.

Elise had the idea her own mother would have been that way. It sure would have been nice to find out.

The wooden floor was littered with colorful rugs. Display cases had pieces of gold, brightly-colored rocks and precious gems. There were antiques, too, in-between. She and Cooper had found some of the paraphernalia. Her favorite was a carbide mining lamp. It had been just a few steps in a cave they'd stumbled across, setting out as if waiting for them. It was their only easy find.

No, the living room hadn't changed much, just a few subtle differences. Instead of panning decor, now there were a few guns. One was a really old musket. She wondered if Garrett and his friends had added to the Smith cache while out exploring the Superstitions. There was an old lunch pail that she didn't remember.

For a moment Elise felt a profound sadness that it had been a text reading Garrett's gone! that brought her here. It should have been something else.

Funny, Elise had expected noise, but except for Cooper's voice from down the hallway, the place was quiet. No television blared, no phone was ringing. Sometimes Elise forgot that the Lost Dutchman wasn't like any other home. They always had guests to trip over, games to play and horses whinnying for attention. Cooper's house had always been calm unless it was time to go on a dig. Even his horses had been polite compared to hers.

"Hello?" Elise called.

Karen came around the kitchen corner, a tissue in hand and red splotches darkening her cheeks. She didn't look up and didn't seem to notice Elise as she immediately turned and walked the other way. Then turned again. She was doing the dance of a worried mother, called pacing. Elise looked down the hall and found Cooper, who was on the phone.

She went to Karen, putting a gentle hand on her shoulder and then drawing her into a firm hug and asking, "No word?"

"None. There's no note, but he's run away," Karen said. "Cooper's busy calling all his friends. Some say they haven't really hung out with him in months. No one knows where he is."

"How about David Cagnalia?"

"Cooper just spoke to David's mother. He's gone, too, although his mom doesn't seem too worried. She says he tends to stay out late on Friday nights. He's not answering his cell phone."

"Garrett not answering his, either?"

"I took it away," Karen admitted. "He's grounded. School and Karl's place are the only two destinations, besides church, he's allowed to go. I figured he didn't need it."

Someone knocked at the front door and before Karen could even step in that direction, it opened and Officer Miller stepped in. "We've sent an officer over to Karl Wilcox's place."

He took out a notebook and leaning on the counter joined Elise and Karen in the kitchen. "You think Karl knows something?" Karen asked.

"No, but since Karl and Garrett had an altercation, we want to make sure there was no retalia…" Sam's words tapered off as if he thought better of what he was about to say. Lamely, he finished with "If Garrett's there, we'll soon know."

"He's not there." Cooper came into the room. "He's probably with David. David called while I was at work, shortly before I heard from you, and wanted to know where Garrett was. I got the idea David and Garrett had something planned."

"I called the Apache Creek Cinema," Sam said. "The owner's checking now to see if Garrett's there for the late show. It's a horror flick, and he says it's pretty crowded."

"Garrett doesn't have any money," Karen said. "He asked earlier today if he could borrow some."

Cooper looked from the phone to his mother. "I've called about a dozen of his friends. Except for David, they're all home. And, at least three of them said he asked to borrow money today."

"So he has money?" Sam asked.

"No," Cooper said slowly and started to pace just like his mother. "At least his friends say they didn't lend him any. Mom, you didn't lend him money, right?"

"I told him he needed to earn it. I mentioned a few chores I'd pay him to do, but he didn't seem inclined." She held up her hand, stopping him before he could ask another question. "And before you ask, I've checked. No money is missing from my purse or anywhere else."

"Cooper, what are you thinking?" Elise watched him pace, remembering it was what he did when he was nervous or worried. He used to joke that, thanks to her own nervous habit, he paced best to the tune of "Kum Ba Yah."

"He has a key to the store," Cooper admitted, stopping just in front of the living room door. "He knows where the money is." He turned and headed for the kitchen counter, snatching up a set of keys. "I'm heading to work. I'll call you when I get there. If he's gotten into the cash drawer, I'll soon know."

"I'll come with you," Sam offered.

Elise looked from Cooper to Sam. Sam was a bit older, but he was an Apache Creek boy born and bred, attended their church, and more. Sam probably did the same thing she did, assess each situation by what she knew and did not know of the past.

In this scenario, Cooper and Sam were friends.

She wasn't the only one affected by the decisions of others, the only one who had to clean up broken dreams. The thought was so staggering that she stepped back, putting her hand on the couch to steady herself.

No one noticed.

"The money belongs to our family," Cooper said. "Even if he's taken some without permission, I'll not be pressing charges. You stay here, field the phones with my mother, and figure out some other places for us to look. Call me if you think of anything. I'll head to the store."

"I'll come with you." Elise didn't ask permission. The way she was feeling now, she needed to get out of here, needed to do something.

Cooper started to protest. Then he nodded. "You might be able to talk to Garrett, if he's there. I'm afraid I'll just yell."

A moment later, she sat beside Cooper in his new truck and looked out the window at the dark night.

"You tell your dad where you were going?" Cooper asked.

"No. Your text wasn't exactly full of information." Elise thought about the two words she'd received: Garrett's gone. "If you want, though, I can call him. He'll get a whole posse out looking for Garrett."

"That's what they did for Jasmine," Cooper mumbled. After a moment, he continued, "Until today, it was looking to be a great week. The best in a long time. Yesterday I didn't even have to remind him to go over to Karl's. He went willingly. Twice I heard him telling Mom some inane detail about cotton and how Karl knew so much about crop rotation. Him stealing from Karl was the last thing I would have expected. Now this."

"And you think he's mad enough to run away?" The truck, even though it was newish, smelled like his old one. She breathed in the scent of the dirt that always clung to his boots after a dig. It was complemented by leather and soap. The way her heart was racing, she wasn't sure if the memory was responsible or the quest for Garrett.

"I really don't think Garrett would do anything stupid," Elise added. "He just doesn't seem that type."

"I don't know. A year ago, I'd have agreed. Even a few months after Dad died, I'd have said there was nothing to worry about. Now I just don't know what's going on in his head." Cooper gripped the steering wheel as he turned onto Apache Creek's main road. Elise had the urge to reach over and touch his arm, try to calm him, but she didn't. AJ's Outfitters was just two left turns away. A streetlight cast narrowed light on the parking lot. AJ's Trolley looked a bit menacing parked to the side.

The place was dark.

"Maybe he hasn't been here," Elise said hopefully. She knew better, though. If Garrett had tried to get funds from his mom, his friends and even gone so far as to take money from Karl, the cash register of AJ's Outfitters was the logical next choice.

Cooper was out of the truck and hurrying toward the front door before Elise got her seat belt off. She quickly followed after him as she'd done a million times before.

"If he came here, he remembered to lock up on his

way out." Cooper turned on the light and entered the room, sounding the bell. The place seemed bigger at night, Elise thought, maybe because no one else was around and the gray/black shadows could stretch even farther. Cooper disappeared into the back office and Elise walked around, trying to see if anything looked amiss.

A long tub with water and fool's gold was against the back wall. Any kid that came in had to try his luck. Right now Christmas bulbs and holly circled it. Books on gold digging and the area's history were in the middle. A few machines were by the side wall. A lonely Santa watched as she made her way toward him. Not even he could manage jolly right now.

Cooper shouted something and Elise went through the office door. He was looking in a drawer and shaking his head. When he looked up, his eyes meeting hers, she thought she'd never seen him look so hurt, so ragged.

Not since they broke up at least.

"He took at least a hundred dollars."

"You sure?"

"I'm ninety-four dollars short from today's taking. Plus, I always keep a handful of coins tucked in the back of this drawer."

"You don't go right to the bank after you close the shop?"

"Usually I do, but with what happened today, instead I headed over to Karl Wilcox's place. From there, I went to the police station. I came back when Mom sent me, closed up and put things away. All that before heading home. The bank had already closed by then. And anyway, I didn't want Mom to be alone."

"With Garrett?" Elise wasn't sure if she'd heard right.

"Alone with all we needed to deal with." He finally looked away, slammed his fist on the desk, and pulled out his cell phone. It only took him a minute to phone Sam and report the missing money.

"Let's go," he said, after disconnecting the call.

"Why don't we drive by the Cagnalias' house?" Elise suggested. "David's the only one you've not got in touch with."

For a moment, she thought he might refuse. Then he nodded. "Good idea."

This time heading for the truck he wasn't in as much of a hurry. He made sure to stay by her as they walked through the darkness to his truck, even going as far as opening the passenger door for her. He'd always done that when they were dating, trying to impress her. She got the idea, by the expression on his face, that he didn't even realize he was doing it.

AJ's Outfitters was the only business on the desert road branching off Main Street. Once they got to the traffic light, Cooper turned right and drove across the railroad tracks and past the park where the community pool, baseball fields and skate bowl were.

David Cagnalia lived just a few blocks behind the park. It was an area of town that could use a little tender loving care. His home was box-shaped, painted—at least by streetlight—a strange Pepto-Bismol color. At the moment, it was dark. The front yard was littered with toys and broken boards.

"What kind of car does David have?" Elise asked.

"He's got an old brown sedan that's seen better days." Cooper slowed down as they drove by. He stopped when a figure stood up from the front porch and walked toward the street.

"It's David's mother," Cooper said.

Elise hadn't seen Margaret Cagnalia in more than ten years. Used to be, Margaret would come help out at the Lost Dutchman during the busy seasons. She'd bring her sons David and Leroy. Her third son, Elise didn't remember his name, wasn't born yet. Back then, Harry Cagnalia had been around. Usually unemployed but still around.

Cooper pulled over and stopped the truck. Elise exited the front seat and gave Margaret a hug.

"Your daddy's glad to have you home," Margaret said. Elise wondered when the two of them had had time to talk, then remembered church. Elise no longer attended, but her whole family did. Last Sunday she'd been gone before they'd awakened. Her foray to Two Mules had given her time to ascertain that Randall Morningdove was still willing to host a riding clinic at his ranch. Instead of after school, it would be after church, on Sundays, with Elise driving in every week to head it up. They'd start with twelve students.

"I think my whole family's glad to have me home," Elise agreed. They weren't, however, so happy with her not attending church.

"If you don't come with us, we'll talk about you," Eva had warned jokingly.

Elise had known the warning wasn't all funny. She went on, "It's good to be back." And, it was true. In Two Mules, she'd been involved in many a teenage behavioral issue, but never had she been surrounded by what felt like family. She'd always been surrounded by either strangers or the law. Her coworkers offered advice, sure, but they'd been busy with their own cases. And, for the last year, she'd been on a first-name basis with the five men who made up the law in Two Mules. They hadn't always appreciated her advice.

But then, they hadn't watched her grow from childhood.

"Have you heard from David?" Cooper asked.

"No, I've called twice. If he's at the picture show, he'll have the cell turned off."

"Sam Miller checked. David and Garrett are not at the movies."

"Sometimes he goes into Mesa or Scottsdale, especially if it's a Friday."

"Where does he get the money?" Cooper asked.

Elise saw Margaret flinch and made a mental note to get to know David and soon. She knew he was supposed to be working for her dad instead of Karl, but she'd not seen him.

"Garrett was trying to borrow money all day," Elise said. "We're trying to figure out why."

"I'm not always sure where David gets his money," Margaret admitted. "I've always thought that Garrett footed the bill most of the time."

Elise watched Cooper give a nod. He wasn't surprised by this information. Before he could say anything, his cell phone sounded. He answered with his name and then listened. "You're kidding. No, now that I think about it, I'm not surprised. What hospital?"

This detail sent Margaret reaching for her phone, checking it, and then moving closer to Cooper with a worried frown. "Something happen to the boys?" she asked.

He shook his head and continued with his conversation. "Have you called Mike Hamm? He'll go with you." He paused for a moment, then said, "Good. Call me if you hear anything else."

Ending the call, Cooper turned to Elise. "Karl Wilcox has been taken to the nearest hospital."

"What happened?" Elise asked.

"Apparently when he heard that Garrett had disappeared, he collapsed."

Driving back home through Apache Creek's main street with Elise by his side brought back memories. Unfortunately, Cooper was too mad and too tired to care which memories came back first. Her nestled against him, in the middle of the seat instead of over by the passenger-side window, was the most vivid. He'd dated since then, a lot, but no one fit right, filled Elise's spot.

Then came the memory of her not sitting nestled against him, and instead pressed far away and against the window, looking out and crying. The memory seemed to go on forever although it had only happened once and maybe lasted twenty minutes.

He wished they could redo that day—the day Cindy had died. But he couldn't. And as a result, whenever he and Elise were together, they were polite strangers with an intimate past.

"It's a spider-web effect," Elise said.

"What do you mean?"

"The single action with multiple consequences, like threads spreading from the middle of the web. Garrett's gone missing and couldn't possibly realize how his actions would affect Karl."

"No," Cooper agreed, thinking about Sam Miller, Margaret Cagnalia, his own mother, and even about Glen Chaney who owned the Apache Creek single-screen movie theater. He'd been called when Jasmine Taylor went missing, too. He'd stopped the movie, made everyone stand up and identify themselves.

Jasmine had been at the movies the night before. It was the last social outing they could pinpoint.

"There's a lot Garrett doesn't know," Cooper said, "especially when it comes to Karl."

"I'll go see Karl in the morning," Elise said decisively when they got to end of his block. "He doesn't have any relatives, at least that I'm aware of—I'll have to ask my dad."

"You might want to ask your uncles."

Cooper remembered a ceremony he'd gone to with Elise. Her mom's family was in Kykotsmovi Village, near Holbrook. He met not just the solemn Raymond, but all three uncles and their families. Cooper had stood on the sideline during the Soyal ceremony when Elise received her kachina. He'd seen her in full dress for the Hopi Butterfly Dance, sponsored by her uncles, looking regal and proud.

"Why do you say that?" she asked.

"It's why I texted you in the first place before I realized that Garrett was missing. When we got back from the police station, Mom and I were talking and she said Karl had a son go missing."

Elise nodded. "Miss Sadie told me about that, though she said the boy ran away. She also said that before that, Karl was an active member in the community—went to church, did volunteer work—but that after that, he became a hermit."

"There's more. According to the news articles I found, Karl's son, Billy, was good friends with your mom. I take it she never mentioned anything about him."

"No, but then I'd not remember something like that."

"My mother was just a kid at the time, and she didn't remember much either because Billy was a few grades ahead. She just said that when it came time for her to date, her parents were more strict about how long she could stay out. Everyone was really scared. All they ever found of Billy was his T-shirt. In fact, that was why I was hoping you'd know something. Your Uncle Raymond was part of the group that found Billy's shirt."

Elise shook her head. "Amazing. The only stories I know about Mom's past, I've learned from Emily."

"Your little sister? I'm surprised it's not Eva. As the oldest, I'd think she'd have the clearest memories."

"Eva tells the everyday things, like how Mom would sing us awake in the morning and how she'd make faces in our pancakes. Mom talked a lot about her childhood. She always regretted that she didn't grow up with her brothers on the reservation, but she also said that had she not been raised here, she'd not have met my dad and then had us girls."

"How did she wind up here?"

"Her mother died in childbirth. My grandfather was a sheep farmer and was gone a lot—but I guess that was the last straw. He just left. My uncles were old enough that they could pretty much take care of themselves. So Mom was raised by an aunt who'd married and left the reservation."

"Who was the aunt?"

"Tia Beecher."

"The principal's mom?" Cooper was surprised.

"I think Tia was the principal's aunt or great-aunt or

something. Once Tia passed away, the families didn't do much together. At least to my memory."

He parked in the driveway and opened the truck door. Apache Creek was quiet at night, only the wind blowing, sending the tree limbs swaying. His mother came to the door, opened it to see who had driven up, and then headed back in.

Elise followed Cooper up the stairs, across the porch, and into the house. Another cop was there, one whom Elise didn't recognize. They had a map spread out on the kitchen table.

"Because Garrett is eighteen, we're considering him a low…" The cop Elise didn't know was talking to Karen. Sam beckoned to Cooper. Elise followed them outside.

"Coop, I hate to tell you this," Sam said, "but the kid's probably been sneaking out for months. What you have here is a window screen that's been detached. Granted, Garrett's got about a four-foot drop, but that's not a problem. He's even planned for getting back in."

Sam walked to the edge of the shrubs that grew against the house, bent down and stood up holding a brown footstool.

"You can't see it behind the shrubs. Garrett's a smart kid. In the morning, he makes sure he moves it."

"If Garrett's so smart, why is he sneaking out?"

"Some kids think of it as a rite of passage," Sam said.

"It's only started since my father died."

"You don't know that," Sam pointed out.

"Was Garrett hanging around with David before your dad passed away?" Elise asked.

"Yes, but not as much."

"Garrett have a girlfriend?" Elise asked next.

"Not that I know of."

"He had two girls in the car with them my first day back in town."

Before Cooper could answer, a car turned down the street. Whoever was driving turned the lights off when they got a good block away. The car slowed when it got three houses away, almost coming to a stop. Elise figured David and Garrett realized the game was up when they noted the cop car in the driveway, the Lost Dutchman truck parked in the street, and that all the lights in the house were on.

She gave the boys credit. They didn't back up, drive away. Instead, they pulled in and parked behind her truck.

Cooper's mother was out the front door and down the stairs before the car came to a stop. Neither boy exited the vehicle.

Cooper waited by the front door, Elise next to him. Karen got to the car, hit the passenger-side door a few times and stepped back. Garrett slowly stepped out. Every nuance of his body was stiff. Even from a distance, Elise could see the anger in his stance. What was going on with this boy?

Then Karen broke down in tears and enveloped him in her arms. A moment later, he was patting her back and leading her to the house.

Elise looked at Cooper. There was maybe a hint of relief in his eyes. Not that Garrett would be able to tell.

"We'll handle it from here," he told her. Reminding her again that she wasn't a part of the family.

Funny that she'd allowed herself to feel like one, just for a few hours.

Chapter Nine

The alarm rang Saturday morning at six. Elise opened her eyes, nudged aside Raven who tended to be a blanket hog and stared at her older sister's bedroom. She'd hoped to be moved out of the main house by now, but the cabin she'd been planning to move into wound up with a guest. They were now sold out, and it looked as if their streak would last until February.

Winter was bread-and-butter to an Arizona dude ranch. If Elise wanted privacy, she'd need to rent an apartment in town. But what she wanted more was financial security. With no need to spend money on rent, this was an excellent time to save. Plus, the horses were a holler away.

Blinking, Elise surveyed the room. It was pink and green, girly, with lots of homemade crafts and books that Eva hadn't packed up yet. One of Eva's handwoven blankets was on the bed. Another one, partially finished, was earmarked for Timmy and on the loom.

Elise couldn't remember Eva being happier.

Jacob had given them fifty acres as a wedding present. He'd promised Elise the same thing back when she and Cooper had been talking marriage. She'd been newly turned eighteen, already wearing an engagement ring, and full of dreams—her daily schedule filled from morning until night just to make sure they all came true.

Instead they had all come crashing down.

Raven whined a bit and jumped off the bed. Who knew where Gray Fox was. He'd probably already headed into the kitchen and convinced Cook to feed him. The dogs had adjusted to their new home better than Elise had.

Elise fingered the blanket on top of Eva's bed. It was a mixture of white, red and brown handwoven by their mother, Naomi. Elise's blanket was green, red and brown. She had no idea where it was. She'd given it to her father a week after her mother died and told him to throw it away. She didn't want the blanket; she wanted her mother.

Even if the blanket had stayed on her bed, she wouldn't have gotten much use out of it. She'd crawled into bed with Eva every night for almost a year. Because after their mother's death, Elise couldn't bear to be in her bedroom alone. It was later, in a psychology class, that Elise figured out Eva's room reminded her of their mother. The weavings, the kachina on the nightstand and Eva's soothing voice. Elise had needed the connection, because at age eight, Elise's room had been one big horse exhibit.

Maybe if Elise's mother hadn't died, Elise wouldn't still feel so lost. Though, if Elise were honest with herself, she hadn't felt lost until she left the Lost Dutchman.

She had a bachelor in social work and a minor in counseling. She'd come to terms with the loss of her mother. Cancer was an enemy that made itself known.

She'd just been too young to understand at the time, to see the signs. And when she'd encountered death again, at age eighteen, it had come too quickly. That time, there was no warning. Just an unanswered text message and horrible news waiting for her in a cold hospital corridor.

Enough of this! She didn't need an hour to get ready, and she definitely needed to stop dwelling on the past. It was time to act rational, get busy, contribute.

Or at least act grateful for a place to land.

She kicked her way out of bed, feeling as if she'd been held prisoner, and slipped into jeans and a T-shirt. Raven jumped from the bed and ran to the door and then back to her, clearly wanting her to hurry. She opened the door and let the German-shepherd-collie mix out. Then, carrying her socks and one boot—which was all she could find—she headed to the back porch and sat down.

Raven streaked across the road, heading for the restaurant. He knew that Cook was good for real bones and meat while Elise was good for chow mix. She couldn't fault her dogs for enjoying their stay at the Lost Dutchman.

Sitting her boot on the porch and stuffing her socks inside, she leaned back and started rocking. The best thing about December in Apache Creek was the weather. She could breathe here, something she couldn't do in Two Mules. Her dogs, Raven and Gray Fox, felt the same way.

She loved Apache Creek. Always had. Her home, the town, the people. The few times she'd attended church in Two Mules, she'd bowed her head and thanked God for giving her a childhood where she'd played, worked hard and was loved.

Then, because she'd turned her back on what God had given her, she'd felt guilty. To escape that feeling, she'd stopped attending church.

Best she not think about playing, working and loving today because that made her think about Cooper. She could manage seeing him again, maybe even take Timmy on another gold-panning expedition. She'd have Timmy to look after, and Cooper would have a host of riders—some seasoned, some rookies—to watch over. If she were careful, she could pretend they were just friends from the same town. He a guide, she a customer.

Two weeks ago had been fun, especially when Cooper got up close and personal with a jumping cholla. But it was the Superstition Mountains that called her name. Not Cooper Smith.

"Hey, Elise, you doing all right?" Her brother-in-law, Jesse, came out the back door. He reminded her a bit of their dad, very focused and serious.

"Not sure. Ask me after I find my other boot."

Jesse raised an eyebrow. "You lost a boot?"

"It's not in the bedroom and that's where I had it last."

"Hmm, could be Timmy's puppy got in your room."

That would explain why Gray Fox hadn't slept with her. He pouted when another dog, besides Raven, got close to her.

"You know where Goober takes things?"

"No, but ask Timmy. He's been up for hours. Done a morning ride with a group."

Elise put on her socks, but stayed in the rocking chair as Jesse ambled off. When was the last time she'd actually sat back and relaxed? Weeks? Months? Years?

The real question, though, was when was the last time she'd had fun.

Definitely years.

The last few weeks, somewhat. Unbidden, Cooper's face came to mind. She wondered how much fun he'd had since their breakup. Eva had once mentioned a girl he'd met at college. Certainly, since she returned, it had been no song and dance for him. Brother skipping school, work, brother missing.

Elise stood and walked to the end of the porch. Raven joined her, leaning against her mistress's legs as if for support. Raven didn't need the assistance; Elise did. Reaching down, Elise stroked the dog's head, and Raven bowed her head for more.

Bowed her head.

Something Elise needed to do. She'd done it for some of her Two Mules clients. She could do it for Garrett. No one was around. It was her, the view from the back porch and God.

When she raised her head and opened her eyes, the first thing she saw was the Superstition Mountains. God's grandest painting, her dad called them. She'd ridden through its beauty just a few weeks ago. She wished she were going again today. She could use some hours getting lost in the wilderness with only the Sonoran Desert and its many plants and animals for company.

She'd once heard an old-timer claim that the Superstition was home to everything that sticks, stings or bites.

She had teased Cooper many a day, blaming him for her scratches, bumps and stings. Yet, she'd enjoyed every minute of their outings, only now appreciating the time and money he put into exploring the terrain and hunting for gold. Now that he was running the store, that knowledge and history had to be good for business.

He was lucky, working at the same place where he'd had so much fun.

Where *they'd* had so much fun.

"Are you sad?"

Elise snapped out of her reverie. Timmy, wearing a blue Lost Dutchman Ranch shirt, stood in front of her. He'd probably been there awhile.

"A little."

"I used to be sad, but Eva said that it's harder to be sad than happy and I might as well pick the easy way."

Child logic but from a child who hadn't had much of a childhood.

"Eva's right."

"I wish we were going panning today, but Daddy says Mr. Cooper only goes after a rain."

"If you go any other time, you've got to carry your own water. Makes it tough." She knew, however, that Cooper often went on his own. He loaded the mules with gallons of water and went off the beaten path and had his special places. He had once found two hundred dollars in gold.

"I want to go again. Would you take me?"

"Your dad might really enjoy taking you."

"Saturdays are the busiest day here," Timmy said, all practical. "And, last-minute is really hard for him. He's important, you know."

"We'll see" was as close to a promise as Elise was willing to go. She needed to avoid Cooper, not put herself in his path—except when it came to Garrett.

If she were honest with herself, the old feelings weren't staying old. They were resurfacing, changing, growing. She needed to stop any new sprout of love before it had a chance to blossom.

"I'm adding it to my Christmas list and putting your name by it. Daddy says I can make two lists: one to Santa and the other to family. You're family even if you don't come around too often."

"I'm here now," she reminded him.

"Exactly why I can put your name by my request. I'll go tell Eva that you said yes."

"That might be a little premature," Elise warned.

"What's premature mean?"

"It means you're thinking something is going to happen when you should also be thinking it might not."

He scrunched up his face. "That makes no sense."

She laughed.

Timmy didn't laugh. "Dad said I shouldn't count on you. That you had commitments elsewhere." He looked at her thoughtfully. "I can't imagine wanting to be anywhere but here. This is the best place ever."

"I'm not going anywhere for a while," Elise assured him.

"Good, because you only have one boot."

He'd changed the subject as only a child could do. She looked down at her single footwear and admitted, "I think your puppy took my other one."

Timmy looked slightly guilty. "He destroyed my Spiderman tennis shoes last night. Eva's ready to put him outside."

"I think I have a spare pair somewhere around here. Go on down and help your dad. I'm not mad a bit."

Timmy didn't need to be told twice. No doubt, even at a young age, he knew women changed their mind.

In stockinged feet, she reentered the house and went

looking for her father. He was in his office—her old room.

"Hey, Dad," she interrupted him.

"What do you need, honey? You sticking around this weekend?" His voice was serious, careful, distant. It hadn't always been that way. It was wrong, she knew, but she'd been his favorite, the one most like him. From the age of two on, she'd sat her own horse fearlessly, with him leading her. He'd let go of her reins when she was four and coordination kicked in. From that time on, she'd been mimicking her dad…she'd mimicked him all the way into the competition ring.

That's probably why he had a hard time forgiving her when she walked—ran, actually—away from the rodeo. Oh, she knew he was glad she was back. Every time they passed each other, sat across from each other at the table, or worked in the stable, he looked her way and she could see it in his eyes. But she saw something else, and it made her question all those psychology classes she'd taken.

He'd never run away from anything. Not from starting a dude ranch with little money, not from his wife's illness, and not from raising three girls—ages twelve, eight and four—by himself.

"For part of it. You know where my old cowboy boots are?"

He looked up from the paper he was reading and nodded toward the closet.

She opened it to find all her trophies, some clothes, her kachina in a special box and two pairs of boots: one pair quite worn, the other practically new.

She sat down cross-legged, pulling both pairs out and feeling the design, hearing long-gone shouts of encouragement as she competed, smelling neglect and seeing the past. The old pair was stiff, cracked and had served her well. The new pair had been her graduation gift from Dad, never worn in competition.

"You planning on sitting there all day or are you going for that ride?"

"I think I'll wear my tennis shoes," she croaked, leaving the room before her dad had a chance to say anything else.

Memories had the ability to lasso a person and make them think they belonged.

When they didn't.

There was so much she wanted to do, bridges to rebuild, but she was conflicted. She'd hated leaving Two Mules. She loved it there.

Loved it here.

And, she knew once she got involved with the kids at Apache Creek High, she'd hesitate to leave because of her commitments to work and home.

She refused to let her mind take her in any other direction.

There was only one thing she could do this morning that would get that man out of her head. Stepping down from the back porch, she ignored the wafting scent of biscuits and gravy, ham and hash browns, and headed toward the stables. She needed to get up close and personal with the wilderness spreading from the Lost Dutchman's back porch. As far as she was concerned, nothing could beat it. The Lost Dutchman Ranch sat on 462 acres, and she'd explored almost every one. It was desert, and cacti, and history. It also held her home— and best of all, the stables.

Pistol was in his stall. He snorted when she entered, causing a few other horses to also acknowledge her.

"We're going for a ride," she told Pistol, leading him from his stall and outside. She checked his hooves and had him brushed, saddled and ready in ten minutes.

"You pack water?" Harold asked, coming around the corner and out of the tack room.

"Not yet."

He pitched in, touching Pistol's nose, and slipping both water and a few snacks in the saddlebag attached to Elise's saddle.

"Wish I'd known you felt like riding. I sent Jesse out just now. He took that David Cagnalia kid with him. First time he's shown up to help out. Jesse's tired. He only expected to do the first trail ride this morning. Your dad was supposed to do the second."

"Why didn't Dad go?"

"First, he's still hurting from when the car ran over his foot last year. He won't admit it, but if he overdoes it, he's in a lot of pain. Next, someone from the church called needing help, and off your dad went."

Sounded just like dad. "It wasn't Garrett's mom?"

Harold raised an eyebrow. "No, it wasn't Cooper's family. I figure they would have called you if they needed something. Weren't you with them most of the night?"

"Yes."

"Guess that's why you need to ride," Harold said. "If I were you, I'd stop running and grow up."

Elise had one foot in the stirrup, about to hoist herself on Pistol's back. She almost lost her balance. "What?"

"Little girl, I've known you since before you could spit. You're going on a ride today because you want to get away from your problems here, as if you think you can outrun them. You could ride all the way to Albuquerque and it wouldn't be far enough."

"You don't know—"

"I know more than you think I know." He shook his head. "All that schooling and you can't see what's in front of you."

Right now, she had a nine-hundred-pound horse in front of her. But she knew what Harold was talking about.

"It's best this way," she murmured.

"For who?"

She gave him a tight smile, hopped on Pistol's back, headed for the gate and toward the Superstition Mountains.

Harold always had a way of asking the questions she didn't know how to answer.

Cooper wasn't going panning today. A dozen people stopped by the minute he changed the Closed sign to Open. Usually it was the hardcore panners and hikers who thought six in the morning the best time to shop.

Not today, when his family was the talk of the town and everyone wanted to look in on them.

And that meant that today, no way could he leave running the business to his little brother and mother. Garrett was a loose cannon. His mother, a wilted bird. Cooper was torn between wanting to lock the door to keep people out or, leave it unlocked and opened—business as usual, only with a more unique crowd. He made two sales, both to strangers. Everyone else wanted to know if Garrett was all right. Most hinted at wanting to know why he'd snuck out. Only a few asked about Cooper's mother or Karl Wilcox.

Elise wasn't one of the people who'd come to the store, and it annoyed Cooper that he kept expecting her to show up.

He was determined to throw himself into his work, pretend everything was all right, and that the Smith family was happy, healthy and…

Falling apart.

"We've a Christmas sale on glass vials with cap," he told Abigail Beecher. She was the eleventh person to stop by, not intending to buy but instead wishing to find out how his family, namely Garrett, was doing.

"Now, Cooper, you know my family doesn't pan. I just want to make sure everything's all right." The principal's daughter was a few years older than Cooper. She'd been a cheerleader when he'd entered high school, and while he'd graduated college and spent almost four years away from Apache Creek, she'd gone into parenthood and was almost single-handedly running the ladies' group at church.

When his father died, she'd been the first at the door with a casserole. She'd also handed him a schedule. The church fed their family for two solid weeks. There wasn't a night when she hadn't called to see what they needed.

Back then Cooper had always said, "Nothing."

He was no longer sure of that response. What he needed was for God to call and ask, "What do you need?" Cooper would spew out, "Help with my mother and brother."

His mother hadn't been able to get out of bed this morning, and Cooper was of the mind that she wanted to and couldn't. Was she really that overcome by Garrett's actions?

"Abigail, why don't you stop by the house and visit my mother. She didn't get out of bed this morning. She said she was fine, just tired, but I'm worried. She's supposed to be here in an hour to take over the store while we do a panning outing."

The tense look left Abigail's face, and Cooper realized that what he'd mistaken for breathless curiosity was really a desire to do something, to help.

"She eat breakfast?"

Cooper tried to remember. "Not while I was home."

"Garrett there, too?"

"No, he's in the office putting together a newsletter."

"He eat breakfast?"

Cooper opened his mouth. He wanted to answer, but he hadn't a clue.

"Did *you* eat breakfast?"

There was maybe a three-second pause while Cooper thought. Then Abigail gave a harrumph and whirled around. Thirty minutes later, she was back with pancakes, eggs and homemade biscuits. "I'm off to your house next. Don't call your mother. I don't want to give her time to think of an excuse not to let me in."

It was early, not even nine. Cooper took his seat behind the desk and ate pancakes while he perused the newsletter his brother had put together. Garrett, now on the other side of the desk while Cooper took the computer seat, shoveled away at his own plate of pancakes. Cooper tried to remember the last time his mother had gotten up in time to fix breakfast. Cooper was happy with cereal and milk. He was usually out of the house before Garrett was out of bed.

"This is good," Cooper said after proofing the second page. Used to be, AJ's put one out each month. It included the dates and times of outings, the price of gold and silver, as well as sale items.

Cooper had managed to get one out three times since February. They had been brief, just bare bones dates and times. Their dad would have been disappointed.

"Did you use to help Dad put this together?"

"Once or twice," Garrett admitted.

This conversation was followed by ten minutes of silence, and not just because they were eating. Cooper didn't have a clue what to say next. He wanted to talk about last night, away from their mother, not to mention Sam and the rest of the police department.

Garrett had been both defensive and scared last night. All he would say was that he and David had gone on a joy ride. "I called David," Garrett had explained. "Told him how upset I was. He came and got me."

"Not the first time, either, I'd guess," Sam had said.

Garrett had the good sense to blush, which sent their mother to crying again. In the end, with the exception of a stern talking to from Sam, punishment had been left with Karen Smith, who seemed too relieved to have her son safely home to consider taking him to task for his behavior. For all Cooper knew, nothing would happen unless he took action.

What had Elise's dad said that Friday last month when he'd caught Garrett skipping school? Do what you're doing. Keep letting him know you're there. Also, when he decides to talk, listen.

"Maybe you could take over this job," Cooper suggested. "We can start getting the newsletter out once a month again. You're better at it than I am."

"I'll do it if I'm around."

Cooper raised one eyebrow. "You going somewhere?"

"I graduate in May. That's only six months away."

Well, this was conversation. Not what Cooper expected to hear but maybe what he needed to hear.

"Dad said you wanted to go to Tucson and attend the University of Arizona. A business degree? Is that right?"

Garrett looked away. "Plans change. I'm not sure what I'm going to do."

"Dad put the money aside, you know. It's there for you, just like it was there for me. Your plans don't have to change."

A bell sounded, someone coming into the store. Garrett took one last bite of pancake and stood up. "It's almost ten, our busy time. What do you want me to do?"

"Take over the front desk. I want to rearrange some inventory. Can you handle it?" Hopefully, Garrett would settle in and free Cooper from the front of the store.

"With my eyes closed."

Something about the way Garrett said the words gave Cooper pause. The kid sounded half disappointed, half bitter. "All right. Good to know."

Cooper followed his brother into the showroom. Together, they looked around at the displays before taking their positions. A customer came in. The phone rang. For a moment, they were merely Mitch Smith's two boys, working together in the duties work brought. The relief, however, was short-lived.

Elise came through the door, breathless. She looked

from Cooper to Garrett before speaking. "My dad just called me. He's with Karl Wilcox at the hospital. Dad says Karl might not make it."

Chapter Ten

"You smell like horse," Elise's dad said after shaking both Cooper's and Garrett's hands and pulling her in for a hug. Mike Hamm stepped forward, too.

"I was riding when you called." Luckily she'd been on her way home, the stables already in sight. When she got to the arena, she rode over to Jesse, filled him in on what was happening and turned Pistol over to him.

She'd already been in her truck and a block away from the Lost Dutchman when she'd thought to call Cooper. Her cell phone, however, was in Eva's bedroom, charging because she'd not charged it overnight.

Too busy with Cooper and Garrett.

"I was at the grocery store," Mike said. "I've got food in the car and can't stay long." He looked at Karl. "Sure hope he wakes up soon."

Elise walked over and took the seat next to Karl's bed. He'd looked old and scraggly when she'd first seen him that day she pulled over to watch him and Garrett. Funny how things had changed since then. Now he just looked old. She wanted the scraggly back. Reaching out, she took his cold hand in hers, noting the wrinkles. He was a man who'd known hard work.

"I'm surprised you're here," Cooper said to her father.

"Naomi was listed as the emergency contact. Not sure how that happened, but she always had a soft spot for him. When they called me, I contacted Mike and then came in her place. It's what she'd have wanted me to do."

Elise looked at Cooper. He'd said that her mother and Karl's son were friends. Was that why? But how many years ago had that been? Eva was over thirty. She'd been born after two years of marriage.

Shaking her head, Elise realized she couldn't do the math here, but she truly wanted to know. "Karl doesn't have any family?"

"Not that I know of," his dad said.

"He doesn't," Garrett spoke up. "When I was over there, he showed me pictures of his son and wife. They're both gone."

"And Karl didn't have any siblings?"

Garrett shrugged. "Not that he mentioned."

To Elise's surprise, Garrett came and sat in a chair on the other side and took Karl's other hand. "He's a smart old man. I never thought cotton could be so interesting. I was kinda looking forward to the season so he could teach me about it." Looking up at Jacob, Garrett asked, "Is he really going to die? Is that what you told Elise?"

Jacob looked as if he didn't want to answer. "What the doctor told me is that he can't find anything wrong with him. His heart's fine, lungs good. Sometimes, though, a man just stops trying to stay alive."

"That makes no sense," Garrett said.

"Then it's a good thing we're all here," Mike said. "If there's one thing that will keep someone going, it's friends. Shall we pray?"

Without responding, both Cooper and her dad bowed their heads. Elise looked across at Garrett. His lips went together for a moment but then he bowed.

Hesitation.

She knew that feeling.

Mike started the prayer, beseeching the Heavenly Father to look down on them, be with Karl, to send him comfort…

Garrett looked up, catching Elise staring at him. There was something in his eyes, something she recognized. It was the same sense of loss she'd been combating this morning. Only, he was so young, just eighteen.

As she'd been.

No, Garrett couldn't turn his back on God. It was too lonely out there without Him. Quickly, Elise bowed her head. She couldn't muster up a prayer, but she could repeat Mike's words as he said them.

The Amen came and Elise released Karl's warm hand. Garrett didn't let go. Turning to his brother, he asked, "Is it all right if I stay here for a while? I promise I won't go anywhere. You can pick me up after work."

"I don't know. The store might be pretty busy. We closed up. People might come back."

"Why don't you go help, Elise," her father suggested. "You filled in plenty of times back in high school."

"I was going to help at the ranch. Cook said something about peeling potatoes."

"Cook's always saying something about peeling potatoes. Truth is, he can peel them faster than anyone else. He just likes people to feel needed. Even Timmy can peel a potato now."

"I can handle the store on my own," Cooper said.

Elise wasn't sure why his declaration made her angry. It shouldn't. He *could* handle the store, didn't need her, but she needed to feel needed.

Peeling potatoes just wouldn't do it.

"Hey!" Garrett stood up, still holding Karl's hand. "He moved a little, pressed my fingers."

"Probably gas," Elise's dad said.

Mike laughed. "No, that's only babies. Believe me, I know."

"I need to stay." Garrett sat back down. "Please, Cooper. This is really important."

Cooper looked from Elise to her father. Again, he remembered what Jacob had said.

Keep letting him know you're there. Also, when he decides to talk, listen.

This wasn't exactly a conversation, but Cooper got the idea it was close. At least his brother was finally asking for something, letting Cooper know what he needed. Maybe Cooper could handle the store on his own, if he weren't already behind from closing shop every time another catastrophe happened.

"I could use the help," he admitted, all the while thinking Elise was the last one he should ask but smart enough to realize by the time he called someone else to fill in, valuable time would have been wasted.

Which is why thirty minutes later he was switching the Closed sign to Open and looking at the notes that had been left on the door.

"What do they say?" Elise asked.

"Two people want me to call them the minute I open. Then this one is from John Stanford."

"The boy from the panning ride," Elise remembered.

"He says that there will be rain the second half of next week and wants to know if I'll go panning."

"Will you? Because I'm sure Timmy will want to go along."

Cooper shook his head. "I don't know. Used to be I had time to sit down and check the upcoming weather report, plan things and get out on my own. Lately all I do is put out fires around here."

"Not everything happening around here is bad. Garrett impressed me back at the hospital. I really think Karl's fingers moved when Garrett took hold of his hand."

It took a lot more to impress Cooper, but he nodded anyway as he led Elise into the store and started turning on lights.

"Garrett just stole from him. Why would he respond to him?"

"Well, for the last two weeks, Karl's not been alone. He's had Garrett there keeping him company."

"Because Garrett has to be there. Community service, remember?"

"Yes, but Garrett's supposed to be there for an hour each afternoon," Elise pointed out. "Have you been keeping track of Garrett's hours? Because, I'm here to tell you, the kid's there two to three hours. Never just one."

Cooper didn't want to confess that he wasn't keeping track. That he was just glad Garrett had someplace to be. Now, however, he understood Garrett's wanting to be at the hospital.

Elise wasn't done. "For Garrett's sake, I hope Karl pulls through."

Then, as if she'd never been gone, Elise went behind the counter and sat on the stool.

She'd just delivered a zinger, Elise style. Nope, Cooper didn't want to think about the guilt his little brother would have if Karl died. The Smith family couldn't take one more burden. It would topple.

Better to deal with the here and now.

"The cash register's the same," he said. "Prices are clearly marked. I'm going to return a few phone calls. If there's anything you can't handle, let me know."

Leaving the door between the office and the front counter open, he settled behind the desk and listened to a few messages on the main line before making the return calls. When that was finished, he checked the weather. Unbelievable. Five out of seven upcoming days had gray clouds and rain pictured. He wanted to think about panning, but his mother couldn't handle the store alone right now, and his brother wouldn't be much of a help.

Too bad Elise wasn't a townie looking for part-time work. He heard the front bell sound and soon Elise started chatting with someone. He stood, leaned against the door frame and watched her answer questions as if she'd never been gone. She'd not forgotten anything he'd taught her.

His customer was a panning enthusiast who'd only recently moved to the valley. The door had barely closed on him before the next two customers arrived, a pair of townies. Both were thrilled to see Elise; both assumed she was there to help Cooper. She easily changed the subject, bringing up Karl's condition. He watched as she walked around the store, adjusting signs and making sales.

Some of the people, he knew, stopped by just to see her. Others wanted to see what was going on with his family. Soon, they were being redirected to concern for Karl.

"Yes," Elise said, "he's in the hospital. We're expecting Garrett to call with an update any minute."

"Garrett's a good kid." This came from an older woman who attended Cooper's church. Outside of "How are you doing?" and "So sorry about your dad," he didn't think she'd said a whole sentence to him in all the time he'd been back. Now she was telling Elise about Garrett helping her carry groceries from her car to her kitchen because he'd been driving by and saw a need.

During the next two hours, he heard two or three more "Garrett helped me" stories.

He also watched as Elise filled Santa's gold pan with candy, took colored markers and added artwork to all his Christmas sale signs, and turned on the radio to a station playing seasonal songs.

He forced himself to stay in the back, although he really wanted to be out front. He couldn't imagine anyone else he'd rather be working beside. In just a few hours, she'd turned AJ's Outfitters back into a family business instead of a business to maintain.

His cell sounded right before closing time. Garrett's voice came breathless over the line. "Karl's doing better. They've still got him hooked up to the IV, but his color is good and he's opened his eyes."

"You need me to come get you?" Cooper asked.

"Not right away, okay? Let me stay here another hour or two."

Cooper opened his mouth to protest. It was late, and if he didn't go get Garrett now, it would be ten or so before they got home. "All right," he heard himself say. "I'll close up the shop, go get something to eat and then come get you."

"Thanks. I appreciate it."

Cooper hung up and realized that it had been a long time since Garrett had spoken to him without an edge to his words, a biting tone.

It felt good.

He stood and walked to the office door, watching Elise trying to make gold-panning Santa not lean so much, and he realized that he was doing for Garrett something he hadn't done for Elise. Giving the boy a chance to heal. Not letting the anger separate them forever.

When he and Elise broke up, he'd turned away, angry, burying himself in college and rodeo and whatever he could find. He'd not let Elise know he was still there and that when she was ready to talk, he'd be willing to listen.

If he'd been mature enough to do that, where would they be now?

She turned, saw him watching her and smiled. "Santa's had too much milk and cookies. He can barely stand."

"It's probably time to buy a new Santa. We've had that one since I was a kid."

"I remember we used him for a rodeo one year. The benefit for Mrs. Cagnalia when her mother needed that operation."

"I remember." Cooper didn't move, but stayed in the door frame as Elise made her way toward him, straightening displays and picking up a penny from the floor, until she finally reached him, stopping just before she'd need to squeeze by him if he didn't move.

He wasn't about to move, not when she was so close he could touch. He *wanted* to touch.

"I need to wash my hands," she said.

The employee bathroom was in the office. He started to scoot aside, let her by, but just as he started to move, he caught sight of what was above their heads.

Mistletoe.

She looked up, too.

And frowned.

No, not a chance would Elise Rosemary Hubrecht frown when caught under the mistletoe with Cooper Smith. He couldn't let that situation stand. He put one finger under her warm and haughty chin and tilted it toward his lips. Then he captured them in his, feeling the softness, the power, the memories of a youth spent by her side.

He wanted to kiss her forever.

Instead, the large brass bell that announced customers sounded. He wanted to ignore it, but Elise ducked under his arm, and someone shouted, "Cooper, you here?"

"Yeah, John."

A few minutes later, John had laid out a plan for next Saturday if it rained. The kid didn't even blink as Elise came from the back room, said goodbye to both of them and then whisked out the door.

Cooper took one step, thinking to follow, but hesitated. She'd been back less than a month, dropped into his life thanks to his little brother and her job circumstances, not because she felt the urge to return home.

And there was unfinished business between them.

If they were to go out for dinner, an idea he'd been toying with before the kiss, they'd have to talk. If they did, their uneasy alliance might crumble. Or, maybe they could move forward. Asking her out meant he wanted to. If she said yes, maybe she did, too.

But what if she said no?

The door closed behind her and John kept talking, unaware that Cooper hadn't heard a word he'd said. Elise still wielding power over him.

And Cooper had too many other things to worry about: his work, his mother, his brother.

He let her go.

Two Mules was always quiet on Sunday mornings. A few people were in church, a few more hungover, and the rest taking it easy or working. Elise drove by her old place of work. Funny, it hadn't even been a month but it looked a little more run-down and a whole lot forlorn.

Her caseload had been divided among the other social workers. They wouldn't appreciate her coming back and checking up on things. So she didn't stop by Tammi or Wynita's place. She'd made a few phone calls and knew Tammi was back home. She didn't have a clue what was happening with Wynita.

She drove all the way through town, getting to Randall Morningdove's place right when he, Gina and Gina's daughter arrived home from church. They hadn't been believers when Elise first met them. Then, when it became apparent that Gina's daughter would be a preemie, Elise had arranged for Mike Hamm and his wife to come for a Saturday afternoon. Mike's wife had brought their little girl, now two, who'd also been a preemie. One visit turned to a dozen. Next thing Elise knew, Randall was scolding *her* about her lack of church attendance.

She hoped he wouldn't say anything today. She'd already endured the probing and disappointed looks from her dad and big sister.

Honestly, though, she'd half wanted to attend. She had a lot of things to pray about. For the first time in a long time, she would put herself on the prayer list. The kiss last night from Cooper had kept her awake most of the night. The few times she'd fallen asleep, he'd been in her dreams. She kept remembering the kiss, how good it had been, how alive she'd felt.

For the first time in a long time.

"Just in time for dinner," Randall said.

"I love your cooking."

Randall was a meat-and-potatoes man but whenever he knew Elise would be there, he made Indian fry bread. Her favorite.

"Look," Gina called, "Bridget's walking."

Falling was more like it. Two steps, topple; three steps, topple. Both Gina and her dad watched as if the small girl was a trapeze artist extraordinaire.

"Do you know how many kids are coming?" Elise asked, heading for the back of her truck and taking out gear. The Morningdoves had a few extra saddles, old but good quality. They had bridles, bits, blankets and grooming supplies. They didn't, however, have helmets.

Randall and his daughter exchanged a look.

"Don't tell me none," Elise said.

"We now have commitments from four," Randall admitted.

A few weeks ago, when she'd started planning this, a dozen kids had said they wanted to be involved.

Elise left the extra saddles in her truck bed. She wouldn't need them. "What happened?"

"Most thought it would be after school. Then, too, they know we didn't find a sponsor. That pretty much means this is just a bare-bones riding school, nothing more. Most were excited because you were going to teach it. They've researched you online, know about your buckles and saddles and such. But they know this is no clinic."

Elise looked around the grounds. Randall didn't have an arena. He didn't have any round bales for the students to lasso, and before they could train, they'd need to pick rocks out of the area they'd use for the ring.

"If they can ride here, they can ride anywhere," Elise said, more to herself than to Randall. "Once we've got the kids lassoing with some degree of grace, my dad will donate a few round bales."

He shrugged. "You'll have to convince them of that. Four is a fine number to start with. Give them the right kind of experience, get them talking, the others will follow."

Elise hoped so.

The official start time was two, to give Elise time to drive in from Apache Creek and Randall time to settle in after attending church. Right on time, they had six horses standing, two saddled and four waiting to see what kind of rider they'd be assigned.

"These aren't rodeo stock," Randall cautioned. "They are good rides but that's all they're meant for."

"They're perfect."

At two-fifteen their first student showed up. Clint

Ouray came with his mother. She dropped him off in front of the barn, waved at both Randall and Elise, and drove away. Clint looked from Elise to the horses and then at his mother's slowly disappearing car. Clearly, he was having second thoughts.

"Clint!" Elise hurried to him, hustled him over to meet the horses. She'd known, of course, that Clint had zero riding experience, but she'd not realized until this moment that he was a bit scared of horses.

Thirty minutes later, they were joined by twin brothers as well as Bernice Sinquah. The brothers, Thomas and Tate Begay, were already good riders. They were here because they dreamed of rodeo and when it came to getting training, Elise was as good as they were going to get. Bernice had not been on Elise's radar. She was an honor student who already had a full ride scholarship coming up. Her parents didn't drop her off. They were standing by the fence watching. Elise knew that if she made a reasonable request, like gloves or boots for the other three, they'd see it was filled.

Bernice didn't need the riding school, but Elise wasn't about to turn her away, not when they just had four. Also, she knew if she even mentioned turning Bernice away, she'd get an earful from Randall.

An hour later, Elise categorized Bernice as a hesitant rider. She spent her time with Randall, who introduced her to Sunrise, one of his best behaved horses. Bernice did everything Randall said, slowly and carefully. Bernice's father could ride. He and his wife soon gravitated to Clint. After watching a few minutes, Elise realized where Bernice got her hesitancy. Her mother was afraid of horses, like Clint was. Randall gave them two of his most gentle horses. Soon Bernice's dad was teaching both his wife and Clint the basics.

Clint no longer looked as if he wanted to be somewhere else.

Elise stood still while Thomas and Tate saddled their horses and waited for her.

Clint was looking at Bernice's dad and nodding, eager to please. Unbidden, a scripture came to Elise, one of the few she knew by heart.

"Be not forgetful to entertain strangers for thereby some have entertained angels unawares."

She'd not wanted the Sinquahs at the riding school. Their daughter didn't need interventions, mentors or such. But maybe the riding school needed them.

"We looked up a roping clinic," Thomas told her. "It would have cost us almost a thousand dollars each!"

"That didn't include the bunkhouse and meals, either." Tate sounded a bit disgusted.

"Plus," Thomas added, "we don't know if we're intermediate or advanced riders."

By five o'clock, when all were grooming their horses and putting tack away, Elise knew the twins had the skill to be advanced but needed some more polish. Since they didn't own their own horses but only rode when they visited their uncle two towns away, that was no surprise. Next week, she'd start their roping lessons. She'd figure out a way to start videoing the lessons, too. These boys could actually go somewhere. They had the desire and the talent. She just hoped they took starting at the bottom gracefully. Next week she'd have them playing with ropes and PVC pipe. It looked silly, felt silly, but it definitely improved control.

Meanwhile, Clint had managed a whole ride around Randall's house. He looked both scared and happy.

Bernice had ridden with him. If Elise had to guess, she'd say that while Bernice was scared of horses, too, she had a personality that wouldn't admit to being scared of anything. Her mother had made it down the road and then had used the fence to dismount.

"Next week, show up in pants and long-sleeve shirts. If you have boots, wear them. Tennis shoes are okay, but not the best."

As everyone drove away and Elise prepared for the drive back to Apache Creek, she felt good. She shouldn't. Only four kids had shown up. But she got the idea that all four would be back next week. That was the best news of all.

She was making a difference.

Now she needed to do the same in Apache Creek.

Chapter Eleven

Apache Creek High School's parking lot was a tangle of both parents arriving to pick up their offspring and of lucky offspring, who happened to have their own vehicles, leaving. Twice Cooper said a quick "Thank You" to God for not getting hit by the fairly new drivers who made too-wide turns.

After parking, he walked through the hallway to the principal's office. Around him, groups of kids huddled, talking about their weekend or about homework, depending on the type of kid they were.

Garrett had had quite the weekend, that was for sure. Yesterday, he'd spent the whole day at the hospital. Karl was conscious and doing much better. He'd probably get out tomorrow. Cooper had no idea where Garrett was right now. He had no after-school clubs, and there was no sense in going over to Karl's if Karl wasn't there.

Cooper wished his next thought could be erased.

If not for the stealing episode, he'd have been proud of his little brother for heading over there alone to take care of things. Now the thought of Garrett there alone worried Cooper. Taking a moment, Cooper leaned against a wall and sent a quick text to Garrett, asking him to relieve their mother at the store.

"I'm here for my three-fifteen appointment with Principal Beecher," Cooper told the school secretary.

"He's in a meeting and running late. Give him about twenty minutes."

Great, twenty minutes more his mother would have to run the store alone. She'd shown up right before he needed to leave. He'd almost called the school to cancel his meeting. Mom had a migraine. She'd sat down on the bench behind the counter and leaned back so her head was against the wall.

"It hurts when you move?" he'd asked.

"It will go away."

"Mom, I can handle this. Go home."

"It's just an hour. I'll make it."

"It's time for you to call the doctor again. This is more than just getting over Dad's loss. You need—"

She opened her eyes and looked at her watch. "You have ten minutes to get to the high school."

And now because of the principal's scheduling problems, he'd be gone a bit longer.

Not one to sit still, Cooper headed back to the hallway, a little emptier now, and made his way past the classrooms, the cafeteria and over to the counseling area. Stepping up to the counter, he asked the student worker, "Is Elise Hubrecht available?"

"She took off about ten minutes ago. Miss Sadie's here. She's with a student."

Miss Sadie loved Garrett. Last time Garrett had been in to see her, she'd sent him away with homemade brownies. She'd never done that with Cooper. All she'd ever done with Cooper was advise him to take it slow.

"Elise went home early?"

"No, I think Miss Hubrecht was heading for the gym."

The gym. It took Cooper a few minutes to remember why the word "gym" gave him pause. Sam had said Elise had gone after the basketball coach on her second full day of work.

The Apache Creek High School gym had been renovated since Cooper's day. It was now in the back of the school and took a few minutes to get to. He entered a side door and sat on the bottom of a bleacher, out of sight but positioned where he could see everything.

A few students were stretching; the rest were doing drills. Basketball had not been Cooper's calling, but he knew enough to recognize the players who were ball-handing as compared to the ones who were dribbling, passing or shooting. Coach Butler was with his team: circling, offering advice and even demonstrating. Sam had mentioned that the man was old, but Cooper was surprised at how old. The man had to be nearing seventy.

Elise was actually stretching and joking around with the players. She wore blue sweats and a Lost Dutchman Ranch T-shirt. Her feet looked small in tennis shoes instead of boots. Push-ups seemed to be her favorite. Down she went, then back up and looking right at Coach Butler. Even from a distance, Cooper noted the I'm-on-a-mission look on her face.

"What are you doing here?" Garrett plopped down next to him.

"Meeting with the principal. About you."

"Why?"

"You working with Karl Wilcox came about because

of Elise's suggestion. The school feels they have reason to be concerned. Principal Beecher called me this morning."

Garrett looked at the basketball court and then over at Elise.

"And you're in the gym because of me?"

Cooper thought he saw a hint of a grin on Garrett's face. "No, I stopped by Elise's office and they told me she was here. Last week Sam said something about her and Coach Butler having an altercation. Maybe I should have asked you about it."

Garrett watched the court for a few minutes and didn't respond.

"I thought you were going to play basketball?" Cooper said. "Why did you stop?"

"I showed up for two practices. Coach and I don't have the same mindset. I quit."

"Mindset?" Cooper asked, now wishing he'd asked about it earlier. "What do you mean?"

Garrett didn't have time to answer because at that moment Coach Butler started yelling.

"Coaches yell all the time." Cooper hoped his brother hadn't quit because he couldn't take a tough-guy coach.

"Just wait," Garrett muttered. "I wish there was something like you had. Maybe I'd have tried rodeoing. Might have been fun."

Elise stopped doing push-ups. She sat cross-legged, watching the court.

"The coach is older than I expected," Cooper allowed.

"We heard he had actually retired, but then he lost money because of some kind of scam and was desperate for work. Apparently, he used to be good. Coached up in Scottsdale. You go online, you can find all kinds of kudos. Even some comments from his players who liked him. If it weren't for his picture, I'd think it was a different guy."

"You took the time to research?"

"Sure, I did. I'm not the only one. Most of the kids here think he resents having to go back to work."

About that time, the name-calling started. It wasn't cussing. Cooper would give the coach that. But it was meant to belittle. To humiliate. The player Coach Butler addressed took one step back. The other players froze, including the ones still stretching. Then the coach took the basketball from the player and started jabbing it at his face. Oh, he never touched the kid, but it was enough to send the kid moving back even more and enough to take Elise from the floor, to standing and then to walking—no, trotting—onto the court shouting, "Excuse me, Coach Butler!"

Coach Butler visibly took a breath. "This is practice, Miss Hubrecht. As I told you last week, if you have a complaint, feel free to issue it to Principal Beecher."

The words were condescending; the tone was mean. Cooper stood, took one step and paused. Two parents were in attendance. He didn't recognize them, but both were heckling her with comments like "Sit down" and "This is how the game works." Most of the boys looked embarrassed, including the one who'd backed away from the jabbing ball.

Not a one of them would stand up for Elise, even though she was standing up for them. Cooper got it. This was a team sport. To side with her might demonstrate weakness. And, it was also a sure way to make sure you didn't get any play time. On second thought, though... Cooper did a quick count. It looked as if no one had to worry about being a bench warmer. If the whole team was here, they only had two spare players.

In Cooper's day, there were a dozen boys without the skill to be starters vying for second string.

"Were you here last week when this happened?" Cooper asked Garrett out of the side of his mouth. On the court, Elise looked as if she might be rethinking her strategy.

"No, but David was. His little brother will be a freshman next year and David's not sure he'd make it with this coach."

"David's watching out for his little brother?" Out came the second thought of the day that Cooper wanted back. At least he hadn't said the first one—about the dangers of Garrett being at Karl's house alone—out loud.

"Yes, David's actually pretty decent when you take the time to get to know him."

"I deserved that," Cooper admitted.

Elise walked off the court. Her hands were clenched and she spoke to herself loudly, meant to be heard. "This isn't how it's meant to be done. You can coach without bullying."

Cooper stood still: watching her, watching the coach, watching the players. Something wasn't right. He'd not played basketball, but he'd played football, and there wasn't that good-ole-boy feeling of teamwork or camaraderie about this practice. Coach Butler might have some of the boys and their parents fooled that this was what it was like in the big leagues, but Cooper had been in the big leagues.

He'd taken a first-place win at the West Coast Roping Association Finals five years ago. Had a saddle and buckle to prove it. He'd done the same a year earlier at the George Straight Roping Classic. All the years he'd trained with Elise, her father and others had been one big toughen-up-cowboy adventure.

There'd been trainers yelling at him, sure. They were usually right. And he'd done plenty of yelling back. He was usually wrong. Especially after he'd changed partners. Team roping hadn't been nearly as fun without Elise. He'd needed some of those friends/trainers to get in his face. Maybe he'd been lucky because no one had added condescending and mean to the mix.

He was amazed that it was happening here and that Elise was the only one stepping forward. His mom had complained about some of the helicopter parents she encountered. Apparently, none were here at the practice. Or maybe they'd already pulled their kids out of the program, realizing that protesting wouldn't do any good. Elise certainly wasn't going about making change the right way, not in men's sports.

"Elise," he hollered. "Over here."

She looked, she frowned, and to his surprise, she headed his way and demanded, loudly, "Tell me you see what I see."

Behind them the practice continued. Her marching out on the court hadn't changed one thing.

"Why doesn't the principal come in here to watch!" She stopped, looked at Cooper and said, "What if he has and he thinks this is all right?"

Cooper had no answer. To his surprise, Garrett did.

"You should tell the principal to look at the team rosters for the last few years. The number of players is way down. Also, talk to some of the guys who aren't playing this year. They'll tell you why." With that, Garrett turned and walked out the door.

"You heading for the store?" Cooper said to his brother's retreating form.

"Yes, but I can't work tomorrow."

Elise continued talking, not to him, mostly to herself. "And to think, he tells me I need to start thinking about establishing support groups and promoting collaborative processes."

Cooper figured she was talking about the principal. Didn't matter. Her psychobabble was way out of his league. "Why can't you work tomorrow?" he asked Garrett.

"This here is risk assessment on referred students," Elise finished, her voice getting stronger and louder.

"Karl's getting out of the hospital. I'm giving him a ride home." Garrett stopped, turned to face his brother and said, "That is, if you'll unground me. Can I get the keys to the truck for something like that?"

"We'll see." Cooper wasn't willing to promise. Garrett might be fine this moment, but he hadn't been doing "fine" for a few weeks. Good behavior couldn't be hit or miss. Turning around, Cooper was poised to ask Elise what she planned to do, but she was back where the boys had been stretching. She had a notebook in her lap and was writing furiously.

He'd seen this Elise before. Once, when they'd come in second at a Prescott rodeo, she'd made sure to research the team that won. Next rodeo, she was on the front bench, watching their every move and writing furiously. She'd wanted to win.

She wanted to win now, too. One hundred percent sure she was in the right. Cooper thought she had right on her side, but maybe there was more to it than what was in front of them. If Coach Butler had been so good in the past, why the change now? It was almost as if Elise couldn't look right or left for comparisons.

In his heart, though, he knew what she wanted. He'd known it since Cindy died and Elise left the arena and him.

She wanted to save the world.

He just wanted to save her.

Garrett wasn't happy, but Elise didn't care. She'd finally had time today to meet with him, one on one, and discuss his schoolwork, attitude and more.

They sat in her office, which she'd decorated with both family portraits and certificates. At first, she'd felt a bit as if she was bragging. But soon, as she walked the halls they walked, she'd realized the students liked talking about her past and her accomplishments.

It opened discussions about their present and future.

"I'm just done," Garrett said for the third time, checking his watch and looking at her half-open door. "It's like senior year will never end. I've got more important things to do, but school and family are holding me back."

He had his fingers tight around the arms of the cushioned chair facing her desk. He kept pushing himself up, as if he wanted to leave.

"You graduate in six months. Surely you know that a high school diploma is important." She'd had this conversation with two dozen students in the last week. All had looked her in the eye and nodded. Yup, they agreed, and even managed to look sincerely engaged in the dialogue, although most had a trail of truancy baggage that also contained drug use as well as very little parental influence.

Only two stood out. One was Mathias Arias, who currently lived in a van with his parents and two siblings. He played on the basketball team and desperately wanted a scholarship. His father had been in the gym yesterday and hadn't appreciated her interference.

The other was Garrett.

"Six months to graduation, Garrett," she repeated. "Then what do you plan to do?"

He looked at his boots.

"Your brother says you want to go to the university and major in business."

"Not anymore."

"Then tell me."

"I think I want to move in with Karl. Get his place up to speed. Learn about planting cotton and all that. If I learn enough, maybe someday I can have my own place, be my own boss. It's what Cooper is. His own boss. I'm tired of always being told what to do. Never appreciated."

Elise leaned forward. "Did you feel appreciated before your father passed away?"

If it hadn't been for her already established connection with his family, she'd not have asked the question during their first meeting.

"Maybe a little, but my heart isn't in the store. I'm not a panner. It was fun when I was little, but there are more important things."

It was the second time he said "more important things." Something had him going, but she wasn't sure what. Near as she could tell, there wasn't a girlfriend in his life. He didn't belong to any clubs, and David was the friend he spent most, if not all, his time with.

His phone beeped. He looked up at her and for a moment she thought he'd ignored the text, but he said, "It's important."

As he read, he grew agitated, practically coming out of the seat. Whatever he was reading had him just as antsy as the meeting with her.

He quickly typed a message and then stood. "I got to be going." Taking two steps toward the half-opened door, he paused and swung around, one hand holding firm to the knob and his eyes a little frantic. "I don't suppose you'd let me borrow your car and go get Karl?"

"You didn't manage to convince Cooper to unground you?"

"He said he'd drive me over and both of us could bring Karl home."

"And now that isn't going to work?"

"Cooper won't close the shop until seven. That means we won't get to Karl until almost eight. I want to go now. He doesn't like being away from home for too long because his son might come home."

"Billy's been missing for more than thirty years," Elise said gently.

Garrett couldn't hide his surprise. "You know about Billy?"

"A little. It was long before I was born, but I guess my uncles came to help with the search. My mother was a good friend of Billy's."

"Thirty years is a long time to hope," Garrett said. "I think he needs to let go and get on with his life."

Good advice—the type of advice Elise needed to take. Garrett had obviously put some thought into his reasoning. Elise was surprised by his passion. And by his intuition. Why, then, endanger a relationship he treasured by stealing? It made no sense.

"Karl doesn't know why Billy left," the boy continued. "Maybe he's still alive.

"Don't you think Billy would have come back by now if he could? To check on his father. Or at least when his mother died." Elise looked from Garrett to the door. Cooper had just arrived and was standing politely outside, waiting. She wondered if he could hear Garrett talking, if he needed to hear.

Before she had a chance to warn Garrett, he said, "I don't want to think about Mom dying, and I'd have rather been anywhere else when my father died."

From experience, Elise knew that a session could take any number of turns. She'd had clients go violent, she'd had them break down in tears and she'd had a few who refused to say a word. This session with Garrett was one surprise after another.

Saying that he'd rather be anywhere else when his father died was an honest admission. The first step in getting help.

"Why?"

"Because then I could pretend that Dad was still alive. Because in Apache Creek, every time I turn around, I remember."

It felt like the breath swooshed out of Elise's lungs, one big release. Hot tears immediately formed in her eyes, pooling as she furiously tried to blink them away.

Garrett let go of the doorknob and said, "What? Don't cry for me. I'll be all right. Man, if you get all weepy, Cooper will think I did something to you."

Cooper stood stock-still in the hallway, his hands

dangling helplessly at his sides. She knew he was out of his element here. At times like these, he wanted to be doing something whether it be riding a horse or climbing a mountain. Standing around helpless wasn't his style.

Apparently the same was true for Garrett, who repeated, "I've got important things to do if I can just get away long enough."

Elise wanted to say something, reassure him, but her throat had tightened until the very act of swallowing hurt.

Garrett had just summed up her reaction to Cindy's death and why Elise left.

Because, by leaving, she could pretend that Cindy was still alive. Because by staying in Apache Creek, every time Elise turned around, she'd remember.

Cooper did the right thing. He knocked. If it weren't for the pink flush on his cheeks, she'd have believed he'd just arrived.

Garrett wasn't fooled, either.

"How long were you out there?"

"Long enough to know I need to leave you alone about college. I get it. Just tell me you'll finish high school. That's all I ask."

Garrett nodded and said, "Can we go get Karl now?"

"That's why I'm here."

"But you still won't let me drive by myself?"

"Garrett, you stole—"

"I know! There was a reason."

"Not one you've shared with me," Cooper reasoned.

"I can't. I promised."

"Does Karl know why you took the money?"

Garrett looked down at his boots again. Elise felt

torn. On one hand, she was making headway with Garrett. Cooper's appearance changed everything, and she wasn't sure if it were for the better. On the other hand, the two men were talking. Really talking. And, she had to give Cooper credit. He was listening.

"I told him," Garrett muttered.

Both Elise and Cooper raised their eyebrows. This was news.

"But," Garrett admitted, "he was unconscious."

Cooper's mouth twitched. Garrett didn't seem to notice, but Elise did. It had twitched many a time during their dating days, usually when she'd done something that amused him.

"Why did you take the money?" Cooper asked.

"I have a good reason."

Cooper just shook his head. Elise, though, watched Garrett. He was standing straight, not fidgeting, but still coiled tightly as if he was about to spring.

Have. He'd said I *have* a good reason. Not, I *had* a good reason, which meant the reason still existed.

"Garrett," Elise said gently, "why can't you tell us?"

"I promised I wouldn't."

"Whom did you promise? David?" Cooper demanded immediately. The tone and words took Cooper and Garrett all the way back to square one. "Is he in some kind of trouble and—"

"No, it's not David. If anything, David agrees with you." In two steps, Garrett was out the door, reaching back, visibly wanting to slam it.

Elise got an idea just how frustrated he was. If he slammed the door, he left his brother and her inside to talk about him. Plus, he wanted to go pick up Karl, and Cooper was here to do just that.

"Why don't we all go to pick up Karl," Elise said. "Maybe we can cheer him up." To herself, she thought, *And maybe I can get you back to talking to each other as brothers. Talking not about Karl or the money, but about your dad.*

At least that's what she told herself.

No way did she want to admit that maybe, for the first time, she was thinking that she and Cooper needed to talk as friends about losing Cindy.

About losing each other.

Chapter Twelve

He knew Elise was annoyed at him. Well, too bad. He'd not meant to eavesdrop but he was glad he had. He'd actually had a meaningful conversation with Garrett.

And Garrett was correct. Working where Dad worked, living where Dad lived, reminded them every day of exactly what they'd lost when Mitch Smith died. He wasn't sure that leaving was the answer, but he understood the need.

He couldn't make the same mistake with Garrett that he had with Elise. With her, he'd let go thinking she was running away from him when, in truth, she'd been running away from memories. He'd not been mature enough to understand even when his dad stated the obvious: Best thing you can do is remain a ship in the ocean she'll return to.

Instead, he'd become a ship, too. Not coming home until his dad's health required it.

Elise pulled some strings and borrowed the school van. It wasn't being used, and it would make transporting Karl a whole lot easier. Garrett got in the back while Elise took the wheel and Cooper slipped into the passenger seat. They drove in silence. Used to be Elise was the one to break any extended silence. Today, it was Cooper. "I haven't been in this van since that day your dad drove us to Prescott for Frontier Days."

"Our last competition." Elise smiled.

Cooper smiled, too, thinking about that weekend. They'd been team roping, the youngest competitors, and Elise had been the only girl in the event. He'd let her be the header. Oh, she'd told the world that she was a better header, but he knew better. He was. Not that it mattered. He'd take any part of the steer just to be with her.

She chuckled, so mirthful that even Garrett leaned forward so he could hear. "That was the year I filled in at the start of the show as one of the trick riders."

"What did you do?" Garrett asked.

"Seems to me," Elise said, "that I mainly rode around the arena while standing on the back of Pistol, hoping that the American flag didn't spook him."

"You were worried?" Cooper didn't remember her ever being worried or afraid.

"A little. I wasn't crazy about standing on Pistol's back. It was a long ways down, if I recall. And being the only girl registered for team roping seemed daunting at the time. I mean, girls in team roping were becoming common for high school and college rodeos, but nonexistent for the established rodeos. I kept telling my dad I wasn't ready."

"No one told me that."

"I didn't tell you everything."

"Maybe you should have." He'd honestly thought the whole idea of team roping was hers. Oh, he knew her dad pushed her, but she'd rarely seemed to need the push. She'd been right there leading the way.

By the time they made it to the hospital, it was after five. Karl managed to finish checking out at six, and they were pulling into his driveway a short while later.

"Appreciate you coming to get me." Karl had been silent most of the drive, looking out the window and every once in a while letting out a moan when the van hit a bump.

"We're glad to do it," Elise said.

Garrett didn't mess with words. He was already around the van and helping Karl out. It was dark, and no one had thought to leave a light on. The early dusk added a somber, silent ambience.

Cooper came around to help Karl stand. Down the road he could see the lights on in the old Simon house. It had been empty for years.

"Somebody bought the house down the road?" Cooper had been talking to Garrett, but Karl answered.

"Some crazy lady who chews gum all the time bought it. Moved in the day before I went in the hospital."

Well, Cooper thought, that made sense. From the first ride, Jilly Greenhouse had said she loved the area. She'd been in AJ's a time or two. He'd thought the vacation had been going on a bit long.

"You need a dog." Elise left the van headlights on as Karl fished out the house keys and handed them to Garrett. Whatever anger or betrayal he'd been feeling about the theft was gone.

"Too much trouble."

Lights flashed in the distance. A car turned down the road, slowed and entered the open gate to stop alongside the van. Cooper ambled over and opened the driver's door so his mother could exit. She must be having a good day: she'd managed both work and coming to Karl's. She pointed to a box on the passenger side loaded with a pan of homemade noodle soup and garlic bread. Cooper almost smiled. Yup, this was his mother, the old Karen Smith, the one who helped with homework and the one who took food to needy neighbors. Only now she needed help carrying it.

"Too much fuss," Karl muttered.

"About time," Elise countered.

This was only the second time Cooper had been in Karl's house. Last time he'd been too upset at Garrett's actions to notice his surroundings. Now, after turning on the living room lights, he couldn't help but notice. First, the place was old, probably built more than a hundred years ago. And by the looks of things, it had not been updated much ever since. The living room was small, just enough room for a couch, an easy chair, a coffee table, an empty fish aquarium and a television. There were two doors. Cooper went through the one leading to a dining area that was taken up by a table with four chairs, loaded with newspapers, spare change and mail. Through another door was a small kitchen. His mother, with Elise following, entered it as if she knew just where to go and turned on the light.

"Oh, my."

Cooper followed his mother and looked for a place to lay the box. Every inch of counter space was taken up by old appliances, books, even a space heater. His mother stood in the middle of the room with a big smile on her face.

"My grandmother had one of these." His mom was in awe of a stove, a fairly plain-looking white four-burner appliance that had definitely seen better days. Cooper had never seen one quite like it. Four doors made him wonder if it had four ovens. It might not be as old as the house, but it was close.

"Cooper!"

Garrett's voice carried. He'd gone through the second door. Cooper handed the box of food to Elise and went to the second door that led to a hallway with two bedrooms.

Karl sat on the edge of a bed, looking small and weak. "I just want to change clothes. Don't need anything else."

"Where are your clothes?" Cooper asked.

"My shirts are hanging up and the pants are in the third drawer of the dresser."

Karl's closet was pretty much empty of clothes. There were three shirts, two coats and what looked like a suit. Cooper couldn't tell for certain, as it was zipped in a dry-cleaning bag. He took the first one and then found the jeans in the third drawer. He had a sneaking suspicion that Karl needed help dressing, and Garrett had called for help because he didn't feel up to the task. Cooper wasn't all too sure he was, either. He'd helped with his dad's care. The last month had been brutal, with his dad too weak to brush his own teeth among other things. Garrett, Cooper now realized, had made himself scarce during those days.

And, during those days, Cooper's mom had been by his side helping.

"You need any help?" Elise poked her head in the door.

"No!" Karl and Garrett said at the same time.

"I think we can handle it." Cooper managed to keep a straight face.

Elise looked from the pants and shirts in his hands to Karl sitting on the bed. She looked hesitant to leave, but at that moment someone knocked at the door.

"Saved," she said brightly.

It took Jilly Greenhouse, who claimed she was just being neighborly, only five minutes to get Karl dressed and sitting at the table. For the rest of his life, Cooper didn't think he'd be able to forget the expression on Karl's face when he realized that Jilly was not only going to help him change clothes but also sit him at his table while organizing his medicine.

And soon his house.

She cleaned the dining room table with Elise's help, and then went to the kitchen to help Cooper's mom. "You've got two great boys there," she said by way of introduction.

Cooper didn't mind being called a boy if it got his mother to smile.

"I'd forgotten how good a cook your mom is," Elise said.

She and Cooper were sitting on the lumpy couch and using the coffee table for their bowls of soup. In the dining room, Jilly and Karen were becoming fast friends.

"I think I'd almost forgotten, too," Cooper admitted, trying to turn so he could watch what his brother was up to. Garrett was leaning toward Karl, talking intently. The old man was so involved in Garrett's words that he ate, as if by rote.

"Why didn't you let Garrett have the car keys?" Elise asked. "It was for a good reason."

"He stole. I'm having a hard time getting over that."

Elise nodded, thinking of her little sister, Emily, and

glad that both Eva and her father had always been there to nurture.

"I guess you heard that Garrett doesn't really want to go to college."

"I did."

"What are you going to do?"

"I'm going to listen. I have to remember that he lost Dad at a critical time and that maybe time is exactly what he needs. I wish I'd done that with you." There, he'd said it. He set his bowl on the table and looked in Elise's eyes, waiting for her to duck her head, look away, leave, as she'd been doing for so many years.

"I had a hard time forgiving myself for not reading that stupid text soon enough," she admitted.

"Mike said it wasn't the first time she'd gotten into a car with Brandon when he'd been drinking. He could have gotten into an accident any one of those times."

Elise nodded, so still that the bowl in her hand didn't so much as shake. He hoped it was almost empty.

"She was seventeen," Elise whispered. "She had friends, a loving family, everything she needed to make good choices. She even knew it was a bad idea to get in the car with Brandon—that's why she sent me a text. So why did she do it anyway?"

Cooper didn't remind her that they'd asked themselves that question a million times. So had Cindy's family.

Elise's bowl joined his on the coffee table. He'd finished every bite; she'd managed about half.

Looking back at Elise, Cooper wished he could take her in his arms, hold her close and bury his face in the curve of her neck, letting the scent of her take his worries away.

Instead, he gathered up the dishes, carried them into the kitchen and walked with his mother and brother out to her car. It took a moment for Mom to get him to his truck in the high school parking lot, and then it was time to head home.

Alone.

After checking his email and making sure his mom and brother were comfortable, he went out back and saddled up. Percy Jackson was more than ready for a ride. Cooper headed for the middle of the arena and tried to remember working beside Elise to catch their horses, warm them up and start roping.

It had always been better with two. Even holding the steer so she could put on the horn wrap was fun.

Sitting on his horse in the middle of a quiet arena with only the wind for comfort, he felt so alone.

Maybe he'd been feeling alone every day he'd spent without Elise.

Principal Beecher didn't want to let the year end without a formal introduction of Elise to his faculty and staff. Wednesday, after school, he called a faculty/staff meeting.

Elise felt a sense of anticipation. After all, some of the faculty and staff had been her teachers. It made for an odd partnership. According to the grapevine that Miss Sadie kept faithful track of, all were surprised she became a counselor. Some were impressed she took on Coach Butler. And none were surprised at how often she was spotted with Cooper.

She sat in the back of the cafeteria, waiting for Principal Beecher to finish his announcements. Despite the Christmas decorations and joke wish lists—Elise's personal favorite asked for No Homework Until July, A Three-Hour School Day and Get-Out-of-Tests Free Passes—none of the teachers were in a good mood as the new governor seemed to be all about budget cuts. Elise heard more than one teacher mutter about empty promises and skewed priorities.

When it finally came her turn, she walked to the front and introduced herself. Miss Sadie applauded, which inspired a few more teachers to join in. Knowing their time was valuable and that many had children to gather, and almost as much work at home as here, she introduced herself and then laid out what her job was and her goals were. Some seemed to think she was something like a student success coach. She dispelled that notion, although she sometimes filled the role.

"I'm not here to get their grades up by helping them learn good study skills. I'm here to help get their grades up by dealing with their issues."

The teachers knew all about issues. Elise waited until they got past airing their disappointment with calling social services to be told, "You're reporting neglect— we only have the manpower to investigate abuse," as well as, "If I hear the term social promotion one more time, I'll hurl," before outlining the kinds of one-on-one meetings she'd been having with students. She then talked about the two programs starting in January— one for students of divorced parents, and the other for the prevention of bullying.

Next she talked about how the teachers could help. "Any behavioral differences or excessive absences, any change in routine, go ahead and stop by my office or shoot me an email. If I get more than one about the same student, I'll know to investigate. We need to be proactive, not retroactive."

"Maybe then Jasmine Taylor wouldn't be missing."

Elise didn't know which teacher said the words, but every teacher nodded his or her head. Principal Beecher stood, coming to stand beside Elise. "Exactly why we hired a school social worker."

Elise's audience was gone. Oh, participation was high. They all had something to say about Jasmine. Elise caught snippets. "Rarely said more than a dozen words in class."

"Smart girl."

"Nice family."

"Should never have put her in a group with David Cagnalia and Mathias Arias."

As Elise gathered up her purse and walked to her truck, she could only marvel at all that the teachers had to share. More than they probably realized.

Driving home, Elise rolled down the window and admired the view. Why had it taken her so long to come home? In some ways, she was battling a painful past, but the longer she stayed, the more she realized it was worth the time. Her dad was nearing sixty and limping from having his foot run over by a car over a year ago. Harold Mull didn't seem to be slowing down, but his hair was full silver and every once in a while she noticed him sit down just to rest.

Cooper's mom was the biggest change. She was in her early fifties and shouldn't be slowing down so much. Elise was sure it was arthritis, but she wasn't a doctor. It was a spur-of-the-moment idea, a random thought, that had her pulling over to the side of the road and calling Jilly.

"Hello!" Even on the phone, Jilly's personality came across.

"What are you doing tonight?" Elise asked. "Because if you don't have plans, why don't you come to the Lost Dutchman Ranch and have dinner with me? We're a dude ranch, you know, and have a restaurant. My treat, if you'll let me pick your brain a bit. I'd love to ask you a few questions."

"Hmm, I've been wanting to meet more neighbors. That might be a good idea. I was just thinking that I'd take some food over to Karl, but maybe I'll just grab him and bring him along. Is that all right? Will he interfere with what you want to ask me?"

"No, I'll sit him with my dad."

After establishing a time and learning that Jilly didn't need directions, Elise disconnected and headed home. She really was starting to think of it as home again, not the sad trailer she'd lived in for four years in Two Mules. She no longer even wanted to live in one of the cabins, or the apartment over the stables. The main house would do just fine. She was getting to know Eva all over again, and Timmy was a gem. One who asked her every evening, "Will you take me horseback riding?"

Last night, she'd gone into her dad's office and pulled out her kachina, propping it up on Eva's dresser. It did exactly what she'd hoped it would do. Start changing the room from Eva's to Elise's.

Elise took a shower and afterward told her dad she'd invited someone to eat with them.

"Karl, too," she added.

"Wish I'd thought to ask him," Dad said. "Not that

I expect him to show. Your mother used to invite him over but he never came."

He showed up this night, walking in sandwiched between Garrett and Jilly. Cooper, looking as if he'd been coerced, followed along with their mother. Sitting Karl with her dad had been a good idea, but she wasn't too sure how the rest would work. She needn't have worried.

Soon her father's table overflowed. Even Timmy shirked his duties as fetcher of water to sit and listen as the conversation went back in time.

Her father's favorite memory was "Elise came out of the box, that rope barrier was wrapped around her leg and down she went."

"Scared me to death," Cooper said. "She didn't even bounce, just landed flat on her back."

"Yes," Elise agreed, figuring she'd not get to speak to Jilly until later and joining in the fun, "and only Pistol came back to sniff at me and see if I was all right."

"You always did bounce well," Eva said as she served Cooper more barbecue and gave him a smile. She wore a red Christmas stocking cap and bent down to whisper something in Cooper's ear. Elise didn't trust her for a minute, but didn't dare ask about the exchange.

"I remember you practicing in our backyard arena," Garrett said. "You used to have red boots and a red cowboy hat. I wanted red boots and asked for a pair for Christmas."

"I want red boots," Timmy piped up.

Cooper laughed. "He didn't get them. Dad said boys always wore brown or black."

"Is that true?" Timmy looked aghast.

"Pretty much," Cooper said.

For the next hour, Jacob talked to Jilly, Garrett and

Karl had more in-depth talks, and Karen sat back and enjoyed, eating hardly anything and sometimes rubbing her hands.

Elise nudged Cooper and whispered, "Have you talked to your mom about going to the doctor?"

She noticed it took him a moment to answer as he was staring across the dining room at Jesse stealing a kiss from Eva.

"Yes," he finally said, "but she says it's just pain in the joints and old age."

"I think it's arthritis. It's why I called Jilly and invited her over tonight. I wanted to see if she noticed anything last night. I thought her being a nurse and all, maybe she could give your mother a gentle nudge about seeking treatment."

Elise thought they were being quiet, but a slow prickling sensation had her turning to look at Karl. He nodded. "Looks like arthritis to me, too. My wife had it. Sure did make her tired all the time. She rubbed her hands a lot, too."

"I don't have arthritis," Karen protested, sounding a bit put out. "Do we have to talk about this? I'm just trying to cope with the changes in my life."

Cooper looked from Karl to his mom and asked, "Your wife rubbed her hands a lot?"

"When her joints were stiff."

"Mom, there's only one way to be sure."

"I don't need one more thing on my plate. I've got enough to worry about with Garrett—"

"Me?" Garrett interrupted. "You don't need to worry about me."

"Yes, she does." Again, Karl spoke up. For being the one just out of the hospital and the one who'd rarely ventured from his home in the last thirty-odd years, he was certainly making up for lost time.

"Karl…" Garrett's tone was low, pleading. Elise looked at the old man. Sometime during his hospital stay someone had given him a shaving. His face was smooth—a little pale, but not so scraggly. His clothes still hung on him. But, sitting there with Garrett by his side, Elise was reminded of a thought she'd had a few weeks ago. Karl needed Garrett as much as Garrett needed him.

"Don't worry, boy, I won't betray a confidence, but I know from experience that keeping secrets can keep you from living life to the fullest."

Everyone nodded, and Elise wished she could. Did she have a secret like that? No, not really. It wasn't secrets that kept her from living fully; it was regrets.

"I'm glad you're here," Karl told Elise. "Garrett has told me some of the things you're already doing, and how you talk to students and listen to what they have to say. I didn't listen to my son enough. All those years ago, he was bullied, and I just told him to man up. It's what my dad would have told me. I know that's why he ran off. One day he couldn't take it anymore. I just hope he's somewhere and safe. I wish I knew. It's the worst feeling in the world not knowing where your child is. Broke his mother's heart."

"I couldn't bear it if I didn't know where my boys were," Karen said.

Elise noticed that Garrett shifted uncomfortably at her words. He was hiding something, and it was making him uncomfortable.

"Miss Elise," Karl continued, "you need anything to help you get some programs started at that high school, you let me know. Having Garrett around helping has been a pleasure. Maybe there are a few more students who'd like to learn about growing cotton."

"Thank you, Karl. I might take you up on that. Dad, I've been meaning to ask you about taking on the rodeo club again. No one took over when you left."

"I don't know, baby girl. Maybe I'll talk to Jesse. He might be up to leading it, and I could help."

"I'll help," Jilly volunteered. "I've yet to buy a horse but it's on my list, and I have the time."

"How much riding have you done?" Elise's dad asked.

"I rode when I was younger, on the east coast. I was best at keyhole race, but I never competed."

Conversation slowed about then. Looking around the dining room, Elise noted that most tables were empty and already cleaned. Standing, she started gathering plates. Karen rose and started to help, made a face and sat back down.

"I'll help," Cooper said.

Together they put away glasses, wiped down tables and put up chairs. Jilly, Karen and Jacob didn't look as if they intended to move for the night. Garrett and Karl had a checkerboard between them and were back in deep conversation.

"I wonder what Garrett's hiding," Elise said.

"Don't know. I'm glad he confided in Karl, though, because if it were bad, surely Karl would let us know."

Elise wasn't so sure. Gaining the confidence of a troubled teen was a touchy venture. Betray them and you'd likely never get that trust back.

"Think Jilly will convince your mom to see the

doctor?" She changed the subject, thinking that she'd focus on an issue that might actually find resolution.

Cooper nodded. "I heard Jilly saying something about medication, stretching exercises and coping mechanisms. Mom was nodding. It's a start."

Funny, it was more than Elise had hoped for. She'd wanted to nudge Jilly into getting to know Karen Smith. Elise had been thinking that then, the two women could talk. But there'd been no need for a middleman, for Elise. Instead, the two women had talked all on their own.

Much better than Elise's original plan.

"So," Cooper said, "you really think that there's a group of kids that would benefit from a rodeo club? Not many of Garrett's friends have horses, not like our friends did."

"We gravitated toward the horse people."

"No, we didn't. We gravitated toward each other. Your dad's rodeo club was already established, so we always had horse people."

Elise had been so caught up in watching Cooper that she hadn't heard Garrett join them until he said, "Jasmine would have liked such a club."

"One more reason to make this a priority," she agreed.

"Cooper." Garrett was as serious as Elise had ever seen. "We have an arena. It's the perfect size."

"We don't have the horses or the longhorns or the *time*." Cooper emphasized the last word.

It took Elise back a decade, to when she hadn't had the time to check her text messages.

Elise was wiser now. She knew to make time.

She just wished Cooper knew it, too.

She kept wishing for the next few days. In the hallway, kids were exuberant. After all, there were only two more days of school before Christmas break.

Elise appreciated their enthusiasm.

She also appreciated the way her talk to the faculty and staff had brought about some change. At least two teachers, both new, stopped by and asked about disruptive behavior. Elise listened and realized she would have to talk to the vice-principal to make sure they were both comfortable with what she needed to handle compared to what he needed to handle.

At nine, Elise accessed the absence list and looked at names, hunting for any of her seventy-plus. With the exception of Mathias Arias—who didn't have a phone—she personally called any of her brood who missed school.

Two names jumped out: David Cagnalia and Garrett Smith.

She was slated to meet with David today. Well, one of the perks of working at a small school was accessibility. She took out her phone and started to text Cooper. Her phone rang before she could finish. Since it wasn't her office phone, she simply answered with a hello.

"Miss Elise." Karl's voice sounded stronger than it should have for an eightysomething man who'd recently gotten out of the hospital.

"Yes, Karl."

"Any chance you can come out to my place for a little while?"

"I'm at work, Karl, maybe when I get off."

He cleared his throat. "I've got both David and Garrett here. I think you need to hear what they have to say."

"Did you call Cooper?"

Karl cleared his throat again. "Yes, but before I could do more than ask him to come over, he told me he had customers and no time. He said he'd call me back. That was thirty minutes ago."

Elise closed her eyes. Cooper and his obsession with time. He had no time to offer his arena, close to the school and teenager-ready, and he had no time to see what was so important that Karl was reaching out.

And David Cagnalia was there, too?

"I'll clear my schedule and be there in thirty minutes."

One thing about working at a school, all she had to do was tell Miss Sadie, who had the office next to her, and then send notes to the students she had scheduled for the next two hours. Surely, she wouldn't need any more time than that.

Jeans had been her outfit in Two Mules; here at Apache Creek High School, she wore work attire—not severe like the royal-blue suit she'd worn the day she applied, but classy and professional. She wanted the girls to see what it meant to dress up for a job.

Sometimes she wondered if the girls laughed when they watched a professional wearing emerald-green silk pants and a white-and-green blouse dodging the cold rain that had started the moment she walked out of the school's exit to climb into a dusty old truck that backfired every time she started it.

Elise laughed. She had a great job, really. She was back with her family. And the call from Karl proved she was making a difference. A dream come true.

If only all her dreams could come true.

She drove by Jilly's house, thinking that when everything settled down she wanted to see the old Simon place. She'd been in it twice when she was growing up, both times clandestine. She remembered fading wallpaper and old appliances, kind of like Karl's place, where David Cagnalia's car was parked in front of the porch. The front door was open and Elise could hear talking. She hoped the boys had a good reason for skipping school and dragging Karl into their escapades.

Karl met her at the door, stepping out.

"It's taken me since I got out of the hospital to talk Garrett into trusting us. He's sure he's done the wrong thing. I hope you know the right words to say."

Since Sunday? Three full days. "You're scaring me."

"Not my goal."

She followed him into the living room where she could see the dining room table with three teenagers gathered round it. David Cagnalia tapped his fingers on the wood, clearly nervous. Across from him was Garrett, looking young and scared.

But not as young and scared as Jasmine Taylor who sat beside him.

Chapter Thirteen

"Garrett is with Elise," Cooper's mother said from the kitchen after he walked in the door. "They'll meet us at church."

"Church? Why church? What's going on?"

"Elise says Garrett has some things to say and he wants Mike Hamm to be there."

He rubbed the back of his neck and walked to the refrigerator, grabbing a cold bottle of water and taking a drink. Smelled like meat loaf. It had been a long day. Only once before had a tourist bus pulled into AJ's parking lot and dispensed fifty travelers all willing to spend money. He'd taken in more today than he had in the whole month.

He was out of fool's gold necklaces. Two of the tourists planned to come gold-panning with him on Saturday. They thought they could convince two more.

"Did Garrett go over to Karl's after school?" he asked.

"I think so. When Garrett called, I got the idea they were both over there."

"He say anything else? Karl called me at work. You

wouldn't believe how busy I was. I never managed to call him back."

"No, nothing else."

It wasn't until he was in the shower that Cooper realized that for the first time in a long time, his mother was smiling and cooking something besides soup. He also, as the hot water poured over him, realized that he was spending the evening with his mother while Garrett was with Elise.

If he had a few more days like today, when work was hopping and his mother was smiling and Garrett hadn't gotten in any trouble, maybe he'd have time to seriously talk with Elise, see if there was a chance they could heal the past and move forward: together.

He'd realized last night that in the last ten years, he'd been drifting, doing everything right, but doing it all alone. It wasn't what he wanted. He wanted what Jesse Campbell had, a woman to steal kisses from. He wanted what his mother and father had had, a life together.

The meat loaf hit the spot and soon he was squiring his mother out the door. When they got to the church, he looked for Elise's truck but didn't see it. Surprise, surprise, David Cagnalia's car was next to Mike Hamm's near the rear of the church. The minister never parked right by the door.

Cooper and his family had been attending all their lives. His dad had been a deacon, mostly in charge of the building and grounds. Many a Saturday morning, Cooper had helped weed, fix steps or even change the letters on the Welcome sign.

His mother pushed open the door and headed down the hall to knock on Mike's door. Last time Cooper had entered the preacher's office, they'd been planning his dad's funeral.

"Come in."

His mother opened the door and walked in. Cooper followed, stopping after just a few steps. To Cooper's memory, Karl Wilcox had never attended church. He was, as always, in jeans and a T-shirt. He didn't look a bit uncomfortable. Both David and Garrett did. They were sitting on the couch in the back of the room. Elise was in one of the chairs in front of Mike's desk.

Garrett stood, saying just one word. "Mom."

"What's going on?" Cooper asked.

His mother had different priorities. "You all right, son?"

"I am now."

"Karen, go ahead and sit down." Mike Hamm motioned to the seat next to Elise.

"We've had an interesting hour," Elise told Karen. Cooper noticed how she barely looked at him.

"The Taylors, plus Jasmine, and Ariases just left," Mike added.

Karen gasped.

"What?" This was going too fast for Cooper. Jasmine has returned? "Start from the beginning."

"It started when Garrett stole the food and thirty dollars," Karl said, making the most sense. "Now, there are some boys who'd steal money just because they could. I didn't figure Garrett as one. But add to that stealing the food and it made no sense. I had time in the hospital to do some thinking. Kid who takes the time to visit an old man and hold his hand isn't the kind to steal just because he can."

"I was out of money," Garrett admitted, "and making less at the store because I was working fewer hours."

"Whose fault was that?" Cooper asked.

"Cooper, listen," Elise said.

"Go on."

"Mr. Smith," David said, making Cooper look around for his dad, "I got Garrett involved. Jasmine was in my science group and, well, I got to know her. She's a good kid. Quiet, but good."

"When she found out she was pregnant," Garrett said, "she was scared."

"She's pregnant?" Karen's eyes reflected her understanding as the pieces fell together.

"I'm the only one she told," said David. "She didn't mean to tell me, but she kept crying while we were trying to put together our presentation on global warming. Mathias, our other partner, wasn't there. We weren't surprised. Sometimes he had basketball practice. Other times, he stayed with his sister while his parents tried to figure out what to do next, where to go. They're living in their van."

Cooper's mom put her hand over her mouth.

"She picked the right person to trust," Elise said, giving David the kind of praise Cooper wished she'd give him.

"See, she knew if she told her parents that she was pregnant, and Mathias was the father, they'd go after him, and well," said Garrett, "quite frankly Mathias has nothing. The family is about to fall apart. Finding out Mathias got Jasmine pregnant would kill his mom. That's what Jasmine thought."

"I took her to a house my dad owned in Hayden,"

David admitted. "It's been empty for years, and I knew she'd be all right there."

"Your family owns a house in Hayden?" Cooper knew the town. Maybe six hundred people continued to call it home and most of the homes were condemned. It was little more than a ghost town that still had a smelter and some semblance of a community.

"Can't sell it. Town's been dying since forever," said David. "I knew where Mom kept the key. She still pays the taxes. They're cheap and she hopes someday she'll make a return."

"I doubt it," Garrett said. "The place is a dump."

"It has very little crime. We knew she'd be safe. We took her food and gave her money."

Garrett rubbed his forehead, looking younger than he'd looked in a while. "She said it was just until she could make up her mind what to do."

"She was hoping," Mike Hamm said, "that Mathias would get the basketball scholarship he was trying for, and then she could tell him and join him at whatever university he attended. That way his parents wouldn't fall apart."

"She's that worried about his parents falling apart?" Cooper's mother shook her head in wonder. "The poor child. Why didn't she tell her own parents? They'd have helped."

"I can't even imagine what she was going through," Mike said. "She felt leaving was the best thing."

"Leaving solves nothing," Cooper said, surprised by the force of his words.

"I figured that out because of you." Garrett spoke to Cooper but went to stand by Karl. "I know how sad you've been all these years because of Elise leaving. I saw how devastated Karl's been because of his son. I told Karl the truth last Sunday. He kept my secret, but every day told me to bring Jasmine to him."

"We went and got her this morning." David hadn't moved from the couch. Cooper was having a hard time believing that everything David and his brother had done had been with the desire to help.

"I think she was glad to come home."

"Her parents are beyond glad." Mike Hamm stood up, looking at his watch, something Cooper hadn't done since he entered the room.

"Karl's got a couple of ideas for how to help." Elise's voice sounded so sure, so strong. "He's going to let the Ariases live in the second house on his property."

"They'll help me get my land together. It's a good trade."

"I want to keep working for Karl, too," Garrett said, shooting Elise a look. "Even after my community service is over. You, however," he said to Cooper, "need someone to work at the shop. Mathias would be the perfect employee. He wants a job and he's fascinated by all that stuff."

"Wow," Cooper's mother said. "You've spent a lot of time coming up with all these solutions."

Later, Cooper admitted that probably everyone in the room nodded in agreement, but he only saw Elise and realized that he could have been there by her side dealing with the situation.

If only he'd made the time.

Sunday morning, Cooper had a hard time paying attention to the service. He could only think of all the people there who'd needed him...and whom he hadn't taken the time to listen to, chase after.

Oh, he could tell himself that in the last months he'd closed the shop over and over again to be there for Garrett, but he'd not done it with a willing heart, more a prioritizing heart.

It was time to get his priorities together.

Across the auditorium, Elise sat with her family. She looked happier than she had since she returned. Made sense. She'd said her goal was to be there when people needed her. His brother and Jasmine had certainly needed her—and she'd come through for them.

Behind the podium, Mike Hamm gave his sermon and didn't mention Jasmine. No doubt the news was already around town.

When the service ended, Cooper accepted the hugs and handshakes that came with attending a small-town church.

"I drove Karl here," Elise said, coming to stand next to him. "Why don't you give Garrett the keys to your truck, let him drive Karl home, and I'll drive you and your mother home."

"He's ground—" Cooper changed his mind. "I can do that."

In the end, his mother decided to go with Garrett and Karl, just to look at the second house and see what was needed. She could organize the church ladies and they'd have furniture and food arranged in no time.

Cooper sat on the passenger side and marveled how time changed things. Instead of a lariat behind the seat and rodeo fliers on the floor, Elise's truck was clean but with energy bars in the glove box and bottled water on the floor.

"I never know what I'm going to find when I meet with my clients," she explained. "Most won't admit they need help, but will take something simple."

Cooper admitted, "I need to be better at responding when people need help."

Elise seemed to know immediately what he referred to. "Your mom said you had a tourist bus full of customers in the store during the call."

"Taking care of Garrett is more important. My dad would have known that."

"Your dad had the chance to learn parenting from the cradle up. You've kinda landed in it without getting a crash course in basic teenager 101."

"I was a teenager once."

"And," Elise said gently, "we made some whopping mistakes."

It was the first time she'd been willing to talk about the past.

He wanted to ask her if they still had a chance, if she still loved him, and was willing to let go of the pain that had separated them in the past.

He wanted to offer her the moon. All he could offer, though, was himself, and he wanted her to know that he was willing to make the time, for whatever she needed.

"Thanks for the ride." He hopped out of her truck almost before it came to a complete stop. He had plans to draw, things to do.

She blinked a moment. Maybe she'd been expecting him to invite her in. He wanted to, but he had something he wanted to do even more.

She smiled and said, "See you at church on Sunday."

He wasn't sure he could wait that long.

Once she'd backed out of the driveway, he ran up the

steps and let himself into the house. In a flash, he was in jeans and out in the backyard, turning on the floodlights and heading for the arena. The ground would need to be leveled, he'd double his order of grain and he'd need to fix up some pens. When he and Elise were a team, Jacob Hubrecht cared for the steers. This time, Cooper would do it.

It was time for him to take charge of caring for those he loved.

He didn't open on Monday, just left a sign on the store door saying Be Back Tomorrow. He spent the day in his backyard, working on the arena. Garrett and David spent their day helping his mom at Karl's place. The second house was barely habitable.

And Christmas was coming!

He did open on Tuesday, because no matter how he wanted to bury himself in getting his arena ready for a bunch of teens and their social worker—whom he intended to make *his* social worker—he needed to make a living so he could pay for it all.

Mathias, a little pale and a lot clumsy, started work at AJ's Outfitters on Wednesday.

"He's still a little shocked about being a dad," Garrett shared.

Cooper figured fatherhood at eighteen would take a while to get used to.

On Friday, it started raining at four, pouring—the kind of downpour Arizona was famous for.

"Are you going to go panning tomorrow if it keeps raining?" Garrett asked.

Cooper knew exactly how much he'd make if all the

tourists who'd expressed interest showed up. It would be enough to buy five calves.

"It's supposed to stop." Cooper took out his phone and checked the weather. A tiny sun peeked out from a cloud above the numbers 65. Not a single raindrop fell.

Yup, Cooper definitely intended to go. He looked up the Lost Dutchman's phone number, called and asked for Timmy Campbell. For the rest of Friday, Cooper sent one prayer after another, asking for perfect weather and an enterprising six-year-old.

Cooper wasn't a bit surprised the next morning the winter sun peaked from behind the Superstitions and promised the best kind of day. His phone started ringing at five. The old-timers from the tour bus were coming and bringing friends. Even Jilly wanted to pan again.

Leaving Garrett and Matthias to mind the store, Cooper gathered the supplies. Usually, gold panning was his absolute favorite thing to do, but today his heart wasn't in it for the possibility of gold.

His mother showed up right before he needed to leave, taking Mathias under her wing and shooing Garrett out to help Cooper. "Don't come back until you've got enough gold to make me a rich woman."

She used to say that to his dad. Yup, she was feeling better.

Soon, Cooper thought that maybe he'd get to feel better, too. Elise and Timmy were standing at the counter, both dressed for a ride. She had dark circles under her eyes but they didn't make her any less beautiful.

"I brought the horses," she said.

"And I take it you're coming along?"

She smiled at Timmy, not at him. "Yes. First—" she lifted one pant leg of her jeans "—I have these new red boots to break in. Second, this little guy wouldn't leave me alone until I told him I would. I've also come with a list, written by my sister. You can fill it later. She heard you're having a sale, and what Timmy wants for Christmas isn't exactly made at the North Pole."

The only reason Cooper stopped looking at her boots was because he needed to see her face, her beautiful face.

Timmy had no clue something besides an outing was happening. He looked around the store. "Maybe Dad was wrong. I mean, it sure looks to me like that fake Santa over there is panning for gold. I could get rich today. I just need two dollars and thirteen cents."

A smile almost made it to Cooper's lips. There'd been a time when Garrett had been this innocently funny.

"Is there room for us today?" Elise asked. "The Christmas present Timmy finagled from me can't be wrapped."

"I want to keep panning," Timmy piped up.

"My Christmas gift to him," Elise said, "is six panning excursions, one for each year Timmy's been alive, and apparently last time doesn't count because it was a late birthday present."

Cooper raised one eyebrow. She was talking fast, stumbling and changing the direction of her thoughts. He understood her perfectly. Some things never change.

A few minutes later, they were heading for the Last Water parking area. He'd loaded Percy Jackson in with her horses. Timmy wanted to ride with Garrett on the AJ's Outfitters open-air bus, which was fairly full. This trip, besides the tourists and Jilly, they had a last-minute honeymoon couple, as well as—thanks to a booking his mother had forgotten to write down—a writer who was doing research for a book she was writing.

"It's a romance," she exclaimed. Cooper didn't read them, so he wasn't too impressed. Elise, however, seemed to recognize the author's name.

She was in her element, helping out. A couple of times she called Cooper over and asked a question. He overheard the romance author ask her how often she rode.

"For a long time, it's been maybe once a week," came Elise's response. "I'm thinking it might change in the future because I'm back home and have no intention of leaving. I've got some riding to do."

No intention of leaving?

Was that message aimed at him? A mustard seed of hope swelled in his heart. "What kind of riding?" he asked, coming up next to her.

"The kind you need a partner for. Someone once told me I had a natural talent for team roping."

That would have been him.

The writer hadn't moved away. "Natural talent for roping? You do more than trail rides?"

"She won the Arizona High School State Rodeo Finals and the National High School Rodeo Finals," Cooper bragged, wanting to reach out and take her hand, turn her toward him and tilt that chin so he could kiss her. As he'd done right after that win. "She was all set to attend college on a full rodeo scholarship."

"*We* won the Arizona High School State Rodeo Finals," Elise corrected.

"What happened?" Jilly asked.

Cooper's eyes met Elise's. Weeks ago, on this very spot, he'd seen a facade she'd created of her life.

He liked what he saw today better.

"Life happened," he answered Jilly. "And it still is happening."

He moved toward Elise, looking into the lush dark eyes that used to promise him forever.

And saw that promise again. "I can change," he said.

"I know. That's why I'm here. Why I want to be here."

"You can use my arena."

"Both Jilly and Karl tattled."

"How did they know?" Cooper couldn't believe it. Just wait until he got hold of his brother. He'd get him a big—

"I've already called my friend in Two Mules. Starting in January, we're going to bus four Two Mules students out here for practice, too. Jesse said he'd help if you got busy."

Cooper would give his brother a big hug. "You can use the open-air bus," he offered.

"Even better." She didn't look away from him, and the rest of the group seemed to fade away.

"You're the only girl I know who didn't outgrow your love for horses when you discovered boys."

"That's because I didn't need to dismount to find you," she whispered. "You were always right next to me."

It was true. They'd ridden bareback, roped and barrel-jumped together. That was when they were ten and eleven. By the time they hit their teens, they were both champions in the Arizona State High School Rodeo and competing in national competitions.

They'd been planning on college rodeo, together.

Then Cindy died, Elise blamed herself and gave him back his ring and headed off to school. He'd gone on to college, majored in business, competed, did well but not spectacularly.

"I'm sorry I left," she said.

"I'm sorry I didn't follow."

"I won't leave again."

One of the old-timers must have seen enough because he said, "Boy, you going to kiss her or spend all day wishing you did?"

"I've never been able to type Happily Ever After until after the kiss scene," the romance author added.

With that kind of advice, maybe Cooper would pick up a romance novel. Instead, he reached out to Elise and pulled her into his arms.

He liked what he saw in her eyes: happiness. Her smile said even more: love.

"When you gave me back my ring," he said, "you kept a piece of my heart."

"You kept *all* of mine."

He didn't wait any longer. After all this time, the spark between them shouldn't be ignited by a single kiss. Yet, the moment his lips touched hers, something slammed into Cooper's heart.

Possibly the piece he'd been missing for the last ten years.

"Happily ever after?" Elise asked when he finally let her go.

"For ever and ever" seemed like the perfect reply, especially when he followed it with "I love you."

* * * * *

Dear Reader,

Welcome to Apache Creek, Arizona! It's really a smaller version of Apache Junction, Arizona, where, yes, there's a gold-panning store and, best of all, the Superstition Mountains.

One of my favorite memories is riding the Superstitions. There's nothing like the mountain for not only history (Native American and the Lost Dutchman) but also for scenery (especially during and after a rain). Like Cooper, the hero in *Second Chance Christmas*, I've been up close and personal with the not-so-friendly jumping cholla.

I've had many encounters—both good and bad—in my life and for that I thank God. He's been there for each and every one. Elise Hubrecht and Cooper Smith figured out early that they were meant for each other. Sometimes, though, the bump in the road is a chasm that seems impossible to cross.

Nothing, however, is impossible. I hope you enjoy their story of forgiveness, healing and helping.

You can find me online at *www.pamelatracy.com* or email me at *PkayeT@aol.com*. I love hearing from readers.

Pamela Tracy

COMING NEXT MONTH FROM
Love Inspired®

Available December 15, 2015

A FAMILY FOR THE SOLDIER
Lone Star Cowboy League • by Carolyne Aarsen

Returning to his family ranch, injured army vet Grady Stillwater is unprepared for the surprises waiting for him—including his growing feelings for his physical therapist. Can he get past Chloe Miner's secrets and welcome a ready-made family?

AMISH HOMECOMING
Amish Hearts • by Jo Ann Brown

Desperate for help in raising her niece, Leah Beiler goes back to her Amish roots in Paradise Springs, Pennsylvania—and the boy-next-door who she's never forgotten. Could this be their second chance at forever?

AN UNEXPECTED GROOM
Grace Haven • by Ruth Logan Herne

For Kimberly Gallagher, planning a senator's daughter's wedding isn't easy—especially when their security team includes her teenage crush, Drew Slade. Can she move past old hurts to realize the future she's been searching for is standing right beside her?

HER SMALL-TOWN COWBOY
Oaks Crossing • by Mia Ross

When teacher Lily St. George teams up with cowboy Mike Kinley to give horse-riding lessons to the local children, her small-town life goes from simple to extraordinary as she falls for the handsome single dad and his daughter.

ROCKY MOUNTAIN REUNION • by Tina Radcliffe

Contractor Matt Clark is focused on his business—and raising his newly found daughter. When he discovers his latest project will destroy the home of his ex-wife, he'll have to choose between saving his company and a happily-ever-after with his first love.

ALASKAN SANCTUARY • by Teri Wilson

Eager to make her wolf sanctuary a success, Piper Quinn fights every obstacle—even Ethan Hale, the journalist who deems the animals dangerous. Sparks fly, but soon their battle will be to win each other's hearts.

REQUEST YOUR FREE BOOKS!

2 FREE INSPIRATIONAL NOVELS
PLUS 2
FREE
MYSTERY GIFTS

Love Inspired®

YES! Please send me 2 FREE Love Inspired® novels and my 2 FREE mystery gifts (gifts are worth about $10). After receiving them, if I don't wish to receive any more books, I can return the shipping statement marked "cancel." If I don't cancel, I will receive 6 brand-new novels every month and be billed just $4.99 per book in the U.S. or $5.49 per book in Canada. That's a saving of at least 17% off the cover price. It's quite a bargain! Shipping and handling is just 50¢ per book in the U.S. and 75¢ per book in Canada.* I understand that accepting the 2 free books and gifts places me under no obligation to buy anything. I can always return a shipment and cancel at any time. Even if I never buy another book, the two free books and gifts are mine to keep forever.

105/305 IDN GH5P

Name _____ (PLEASE PRINT)

Address _____ Apt. #

City _____ State/Prov. _____ Zip/Postal Code

Signature (if under 18, a parent or guardian must sign)

Mail to the **Reader Service**:
IN U.S.A.: P.O. Box 1867, Buffalo, NY 14240-1867
IN CANADA: P.O. Box 609, Fort Erie, Ontario L2A 5X3

**Are you a subscriber to Love Inspired® books
and want to receive the larger-print edition?
Call 1-800-873-8635 or visit www.ReaderService.com.**

* Terms and prices subject to change without notice. Prices do not include applicable taxes. Sales tax applicable in N.Y. Canadian residents will be charged applicable taxes. Offer not valid in Quebec. This offer is limited to one order per household. Not valid for current subscribers to Love Inspired books. All orders subject to credit approval. Credit or debit balances in a customer's account(s) may be offset by any other outstanding balance owed by or to the customer. Please allow 4 to 6 weeks for delivery. Offer available while quantities last.

Your Privacy—The Reader Service is committed to protecting your privacy. Our Privacy Policy is available online at www.ReaderService.com or upon request from the Reader Service.

We make a portion of our mailing list available to reputable third parties that offer products we believe may interest you. If you prefer that we not exchange your name with third parties, or if you wish to clarify or modify your communication preferences, please visit us at www.ReaderService.com/consumerchoice or write to us at Reader Service Preference Service, P.O. Box 9062, Buffalo, NY 14240-9062. Include your complete name and address.

LI15

"In spite of what she said, my niece knows I love her, and she's already beginning to love her family here. Mandy will adjust soon to the Amish way of life."

"And what about you?"

Leah frowned at Ezra. "What do you mean? I'm happy to be back home, and I don't have much to adjust to other than the quiet at night. Philadelphia was noisy."

"I wasn't talking about that." He hesitated, not sure how to say what he wanted without hurting her feelings.

"Oh." Her smile returned, but it was unsteady. "You're talking about us. We aren't *kinder* any longer, Ezra. I'm sure we can be reasonable about this strange situation we find ourselves in," she said in a tone that suggested she wasn't as certain as she sounded. Uncertain of him or of herself?

"I agree."

"We are neighbors again. We're going to see each other regularly, but it'd be better if we keep any encounters to a minimum." She faltered before hurrying on. "Who knows?

We may even call each other friend again someday. But until then, it'd probably be for the best if you live your life and I live mine." She backed away. "Speaking of that, I need to go and console Mandy." Taking one step, she halted. "*Danki* for letting her name the cow. That made her happier than I've seen her since…"

She didn't finish. She didn't have to. His heart cramped as he thought of the sorrow haunting both Leah and Mandy. They had both lost someone very dear to them, the person Leah had once described to him as "the other half of myself."

The very least he could do was agree to her request that was to everyone's benefit. Even though he knew she was right, he also knew there was no way he could ignore Leah Beiler.

Yet, somehow, he needed to figure out how to do exactly that.

Don't miss
AMISH HOMECOMING by Jo Ann Brown,
available January 2016 wherever
Love Inspired® books and ebooks are sold.